# PAYMENT IN FULL

Lubeck was the first to voice alarm as the house became visible a block away, blazing with lights. Tony quickly undid himself from Marian's embrace.

"Let's go! Fast, Harry, fast! I can smell trouble."

Tony got to the closet first and spied Warren's note.

*I acknowledge payment of cash stolen from my account—$47,000. And for the theft of one slightly used wife—$198,000. Is she worth it, Tony?*

Tony tore open the closet door. "Gone!" he thundered. He turned on Marian. "You!" he shouted. You're the cause of this. Your lousy husband took a quarter million bucks!"

He advanced two steps and walloped her across the face. Marian fell to the floor, whimpering.

"All right," he said, menacingly. "You're going to help me get that dough back. Then I'm gonna do you just one more favor—I'm gonna make you a *widow!*"

## AUTHOR'S PROFILE

Robert Colby was born in New York City, attended a public high school and then went to Mercer Junior College.

During World War II he served with the infantry and saw action in the Marshall and Gilbert Islands, as well as at Saipan and Okinawa.

He was a radio and TV announcer for 15 years with NBC and Mutual in New York and with CBS in Hollywood. Mr. Colby is the author of 11 published novels, among them, KIM and BEAUTIFUL BUT BAD, both Monarch bestsellers.

# The Faster She Runs

Robert Colby

PROLOGUE BOOKS

F + W Media, Inc.

Published in electronic format by
PROLOGUE BOOKS
an imprint of F+W Media, Inc.
10151 Carver Road
Blue Ash, Ohio 45242
*www.prologuebooks.com*

eISBN 10: 1-4405-3922-7
eISBN 13: 978-1-4405-3922-0
POD ISBN 10: 1-4405-5803-5
POD ISBN 13: 978-1-4405-5803-0

This is a work of fiction. Names, characters, corporations, institutions, organizations, events, or locales in this novel are either the product of the author's imagination or, if real, used fictitiously. The resemblance of any character to actual persons (living or dead) is entirely coincidental.

This work has been previously published in print format by:
Monarch Books, Inc., Derby, CT.

# – ONE –

IT WAS JUST A SMALL ARGUMENT, of no real importance by itself. But later that morning Warren Emrick's wife was suddenly confronted by an evil temptation. And because of the argument she was in a mood to betray him. . . .

During the night a December snow had flaked down steadily outside the bedroom windows of their Jackson Heights apartment, covering the ugly truth of broken pavement, barren trees and drab buildings with the bland, white lie of purity.

"I think you're making a mistake," said Warren. "You played sick once before this month and now you want to fake-off from work again. Why? What're you celebrating this time?"

"I'm celebrating boredom," said Marian wearily from her supine position on the bed.

"Boredom!" Warren snorted. "If I took off every time I was bored they'd only see me at the office on payday."

Wearing only pajamas, he stood with his back to her, sipping coffee, gazing down from a window of their bedroom, a lithe muscular man of thirty-four with dark hair crowning features of intense good-looks and mobility.

Absently he followed the movements of two kids who just then stepped into the cold gray light of the street before a yellow-brick apartment house. They carried sleds but set them aside and began to pelt each other with snowballs.

"Proctor's out of town again," said Marian.

"So?"

"So, when he's out of town there's nothing for me to do but study my navel. Or answer the phone. He's got two other girls to take his messages. That's all they're good for anyway."

Marian was Floyd Proctor's private secretary. He was president of Proctor Drugstores, a large cut-rate chain which sold practically anything—even drugs. Warren had to admit, though only to himself, that she was Proctor's spoiled favorite and could do no wrong.

"Well, you're going to get yourself fired," he said over his shoulder. "Sooner or later you'll get caught and then—chop!—no job."

"Don't be silly, Warren," she snapped. "You know that's ridiculous! No matter what I do or don't, I'll be Floyd's girl until—until I begin to look like his wife."

He turned quickly, spilling coffee. "Just as long as you don't *act* like his wife!" Immediately he regretted the remark because he disliked showing his jealousy, losing face with her and with himself. Besides, Proctor was a squat, balding bulb of a man, hardly competition.

"His son is more my style, and my age, wouldn't you say, darling?" She smiled, giving the smile a hint of sly meaning to needle him.

With languid ease she climbed out of bed and stood stretching luxuriously, a rather tall auburn-haired woman of twenty-eight with bold breasts and the long, slim, tapered lines of the truly classic figure.

She was one of those rare types who had no harsh incongruities of structure to argue against her femininity. Her body was a statement: I am woman, I am all woman, every curve, thrust and valley of me is woman.

Yet, in the very perfect symmetry of that physique

there was a loss of identity, of character. Too often one saw the body and not the person.

The face was not quite so perfect. The lips were too heavy, the jaw too pushy, the eyes too gemlike —coldly bright as emeralds, shrewd as money.

"Oh, forget the stupid job," she said, fluffing her hair and moving toward him. "We don't need the income, do we?"

"We?" Warren made a sarcastic face. "No, *we* don't need the income. But you do." He placed the coffee cup and saucer on a table. "Have I ever asked you to contribute a penny of that hundred a week?"

She approached, her breasts extending tautly beneath the frail cover of a pink nightgown. She laced her fingers behind his neck. Her face pouty, she said, "Well, why should I use my few dollars when we have thousands in the bank, honey?"

"Those thousands are for investments," he said firmly, pulling away. "Money to make money. I've told you that a dozen times."

He was a quite successful broker, and for years he had been buying up sound stocks of his own and selling them with a neat margin of profit. He was building capital for a coup that would give him independence for a lifetime. But presently the market was erratic, plunging to a new low. And he had liquidated most of his holdings to await a more certain time. Ninety per cent of his capital rested in a savings account.

"Investments!" Marian sneered. "That's just a name. What's it got to do with pretty clothes, dreamy cars and a cushy little house farther out on the Island, away from this dumpy apartment on this dumpy street? You can play Monopoly with stocks anytime, darling. Let's live it up—now. Now, while the fever's in the blood! Know what I mean?" She moved closer,

7

smoothing an imaginary wrinkle from his pajama pocket.

"Sure, I understand you, Marian. You've got the childish urge to fling it all down the drain in one big the-hell-with-tomorrow orgy of spending. And that's just the attitude which separates the men from the boys, the women from the girls. A little patience and you'll be able to have the same fling with plenty to spare.

"Now—you can quit the job if you like, or you can get yourself canned. But remember, that's a hundred less a week for trinkets and coffee. I can't afford to make up the difference right now."

"Honestly, sweetie," she said. "You're a real old fuddy-duddy sometimes. A regular tightwad." She smiled wryly and mussed his hair in a gesture intended to remove the sting from the remark.

Warren did not believe that he was a tightwad. On the other hand, he knew that he had an obsessive interest in the accumulation of money. This was because he had lived in the grubby, snarling environment of poverty all of his youth. His father had been a short-order cook, a semidrunk who deserted his mother and the hovel in which they lived when Warren was twelve, never to return.

Warren's mother had a slim education and no special skills. She had been forced to take a job as a common waitress in a round-the-clock diner, standing for long night hours on her feet, stumbling home to fall in a stupor upon the lumpy mattress of her sagging bed.

When she wasn't weeping over her fate, she stormed about the tiny house with its junk-sale furniture, scrubbing, ironing, sewing as she screamed abuse at Warren and his older brother.

Warren had caught the disease of her bitterness. He became wrapped in his own little bomb of smoldering rage, exploding his anger with hurtling fists in the littered streets and shabby schoolyards of his limited domain. To create a few dollars out of pennies he sold newspapers, ran errands and poked about the neighborhood for hours, gathering discarded pop bottles for their return deposit.

He grew up with the driving urge to outfight, outsell and outthink his competitors so that he would never again be trapped in the stink and want and groveling degradation of poverty. He came to manhood with the same iron determination to win and hold his winnings, with the same hair-trigger temper in defiance of his enemies.

Only after he had worked his way through college, boxed his way to Golden Gloves Champion, did he learn to smooth the rough edges of his personality, to understand the more subtle approach to human relations.

Yet beneath the velvet cloak of good manners and diplomacy which he now wore, there was always the steel-hard core of himself, primed to resist the slightest threat to the security he had so shrewdly built, the savings he had so carefully stored over the years.

But now Marian was mussing his hair and pressing herself teasingly against him. And he felt a surge of desire which, clouding his better judgment, made him want to placate her.

"All right," he said. "Maybe we'll break loose a bit, toss a few bucks into a new car. After the first of the year, when we get the interest on savings. And remember, Christmas is coming in a few days, honey. Santa has an oversized stocking with your name on it. I have that on good authority—right from the reindeer's mouth."

She gave him a little-girl-pleased smile and he kissed her shoulder. His lips slid downward, seeking, searching. There was anticipation in the slight up-

9

tempo of her breathing, and so he maneuvered her arms from the straps of the gown, pulling it away from her breasts.

He guided her toward the bed, sat down so that she hovered above him. He stared. And stared. . .

"God," he groaned. "Goddamn. What a pair! I never get tired looking at them. I never get enough with you."

She chuckled deep in her throat—all woman now, sure of herself, sure of her power. She cupped her breasts, lifting them, offering them with a cunning, watchful expression. Then, as he was about to grab her, she stepped back out of range. Posing provocatively, she arched her back in a way that caused her breasts to rise and thrust still more invitingly.

At the same time she sucked in her tummy and rotated her torso suggestively. The gown descended and when it clung to her hips she did a little shimmy that sent it slithering to the floor at her feet.

Now she stood naked before him, wearing only the sly ancient smile of the knowing female. With feline grace, she floated back to him. Bending, she ran her soft hands over his body, artfully teasing, goading his hunger.

Trembling with the need of her, he clutched her breasts, kissing the nipples, pressing them against his eyes, his cheeks. Then he pulled her down on top of him and began to stroke the high curve of buttocks, caressing all the warm nakedness of her back.

"Darling, darling," she murmured. "Take the day off and we'll make it a ritual, an all-day production."

"Yes," he answered. "Yes, all right. Okay, hon, maybe I'll spend the whole day with you. Sure I— I'll just do that. God, how I love you! And what's it all for if we don't have time for each other?"

"Ahh, that's my angel, that's my baby," she

soothed. And falling momentarily away from him, began to unbutton his pajamas with long frantic fingers.

But shortly after eight o'clock he glanced at his watch, climbed out of bed and moved briskly toward the bathroom.

"What's the matter?" she called after him.

He turned. "Matter? Why, nothing. Running late, that's all. Make me another cup of java while I shower and throw myself together, will ya, honey?"

"I thought you were going to take the day off," she said peevishly.

It had never occurred to him that she would take seriously what was said in a mindless moment of passion. He felt defensive, seeing no reason for her annoyance, but still not wanting to leave her in a small stew of resentment.

"Well, now, listen, sweetheart, let's be practical. Sure, I'd love to shove the work and spend the whole damn day with you, uninterrupted. It was a terrific idea. Great. But I'm afraid I just didn't think it out. I've got at least three important clients to see and they can't be brushed. The market's about as stable as a glider in a tornado, and these guys just won't let anyone else carry the ball for them in a losing game with all their chips in the pot. I'll have to be there with sharp advice and a crying towel or lose the accounts. Please try to understand."

"I understand all right," she said testily.

"You sound understanding. Oh, very! Well, my job isn't like yours. I can't goof off. The stakes are too high. And anyway, I'm hustling for your goodies as well as my own."

"I understand," she repeated, lighting a cigarette, pushing an angry jet of smoke from the side of her mouth. "I understand that when your belly is full you're no longer interested in the cook until you're hungry again."

"Oh crap, crap! Pure female-type crap, the whining voice of women everywhere, feeling abused, feeling sorry for themselves because they gave it away before they bargained some sucker out of a reward. Well, payment deferred! I'm still late for the office."

He wheeled about and shoved into the bathroom. The ash tray she hurled shattered against the door just as he slammed it.

He came out fifteen minutes later feeling refreshed and a little sorry. After all, there was a certain truth in what she said about the full belly, and he was nudged by a small finger of guilt. Though nothing could have kept him from the ticker tape on such a day.

To his relief she was not in the bedroom, and he was able to dress quickly, undisturbed.

He found her in the kitchen, wearing her pale blue, gold-figured Capri outfit, the one he had bought her only last week on a whim. He was always buying her things without need of a special occasion. It gave him real pleasure. For though they battled frequently, he loved her none the less.

She was smoking moodily, huddled over a cup of coffee. She had not poured one for him.

"I don't know who should be sorry," he said. "Probably me. Please forget the whole stupid bit. Okay, sweetheart?" He leaned down and kissed her cheek. She was unresponsive.

"Before you go, Warren," she said coolly, "would you please phone me in sick? Because I really am sick. Sick, sick, sick!"

"I'd rather not if you don't mind." His temper was rising again. "I'm not much good at these little charades of deceit. They'd know I was lying. Anyway, I haven't time."

"Never mind," she said. "I'll have the maid do it. This is her day to clean."

She went with him to the door, stood silently, grimly, while he got his coat and hat from the hall closet, wrestled them on quickly because now he wanted to escape. It would all be forgotten by dinnertime.

He had his mind on the doorknob and was about to leave with some meaningless parting crack, when suddenly her expression changed to one of mollifying semisweetness. *All is forgiven*, her look said, *though you know you were wrong and I'm being very generous.*

"Have a good day, darling," she cooed, fingering the lapel of his coat. "And try to make it home right around six because I'm doing a roast and I'll time it so we can swallow a couple of martinis first. Sound good?"

"Delicious," he answered. "You're a doll and I'm a brute. I'll make it up to you." He kissed her puckered lips and opened the door. He stepped out.

"Oh! Wait a minute, darling," she cried in an afterthought tone of voice. "Could you let me have fifty until payday? I'm running a little short."

"Fifty?" he repeated. "Sure."

He took her hand, reached into his change pocket, produced a half dollar and slapped it into her palm. He made as if to leave.

"That's funny, Warren," she said. "But not very."

"Last week you were also short," he complained. "So I gave you fifty—until payday. Remember? But I guess you didn't get paid because the subject was dropped, along with the money. What's the trouble, Marian? Betting the horses again? What's good in the third at Santa Anita, Marian?"

13

"Oh, shut up!" she screamed. "Fall under a truck! Drop dead!" She slammed the door in his face.

He stomped off to the elevator and jabbed the button furiously.

*Damn, damn and goddamn!*" he thought. No doubt about it, her face was a red neon confession. She's found another bookie. She can't spend it fast enough, she has to feed it to the ponies.

Okay. He stepped into the elevator, tightening his jaw. Okay, lover-girl, but not from my pocket, not with my money. Not one lousy dollar!

Just wait and see.

14

# – TWO –

MARIAN PLOUGHED INTO THE LIVING ROOM and plucked a cigarette from the silver box on the coffee table. Her hand trembled with anger as she lighted it.

*I'll show him!* she thought. *I'll show the bastard! Wait'll the next time he wants to play love games. I'll yawn right in his face. Miser! Fifty crumby little dollars, that's all. And he's got forty-eight thousand in the bank. Imagine! Well, my turn is coming, Warren. You're in for a hard time, sweetie. Oh, are you ever!*

She fell into a chair, her face brooding, sullen. She began to think about the immediate problem, worrying it, grinding her lip between her teeth.

She was now three-hundred-twenty in the hole to Frank Killian, the bookie who operated from the restaurant in the building where she worked. She had been stalling him, but today was the absolute deadline. He would send a runner to her office or he would come himself. And that was why she had to phone in sick.

She knew what Killian would say: "You get up that dough, girlie. Today! Or I'll drop around to your hubby's office and have a little chat with him—see what I mean? And if that don't work, I got other ways that will."

He'd do it, too. He'd go over to Warren's office and make a big noise. Warren would probably throw him out with a threat to call the police, which wouldn't scare Killian (now and then he paid a fine and went right on booking) but would only cause

15

him to find one of those "other ways" to torture her.

And when Warren got home that night, there would be such a scene—the very thought of it made her cringe.

There was another bookie, a bartender in Jackson Heights. But he was strictly cash. That was why she needed the fifty. If she could have placed a winning bet with the bartender at six to one, she would have been able to pay Killian the next day.

Now what else could she do? Warren put three hundred in her personal checking account every month—her allowance whether she worked or not. But at the moment there were just six dollars and change in the account. The real money was held in savings jointly, though withdrawals required both their signatures.

Big deal! It was supposed to be an honor—share and share alike. Yet Warren would have to die before she could get a penny of that forty-eight thousand for herself.

She could write a personal check, but it would bounce. Then why not write several checks, cashing them at different places, depositing the money, borrowing from Peter to pay Paul, meanwhile betting in the hope of recovering herself?

Yet, where would the cycle end? Right in Warren's lap—unless she hit the jackpot. And she had a secret doubt of this. Everything was going against her lately. The tide was rushing in the wrong direction, hurtling her toward a giant fall.

Her thoughts went round and round, but she could resolve nothing. There was only the diamond ring Warren had given her. She might have to pawn it. And God help her if he noticed it was missing, as he certainly would in short order.

All this trouble because he was so damn stingy.

He was stingy and he was a liar. *Okay hon, maybe I'll spend the whole day with you.* Liar!

She got up and went into the bathroom. She ran water in the tub and peeled off the nightgown, posing herself in front of the full-length mirror behind the door.

*Not bad,* she thought. *Oh, not bad at all, Marian, girl.* She ran her hands upward over long supple thighs and flat tummy to the proud bursting cones of her breasts. *Marvelous, marvelous,* she thought. *In the whole city of New York there probably aren't a dozen figures as beautiful as mine. It's a good face, too. Striking. Yes, striking!*

*I could have any man, absolutely any man I want —anywhere! Remember that, Warren. Any man at all. Yes, and rich ones too. I could take Proctor away from his wife—like that! With a snap of my fingers. If I could only stand him. If I could only have him without letting him touch me. Ugh! Oh, why can't I sell what I've got to the highest bidder? Why was I born with such a weak stomach for ugly sexless men and such a big hunger for the best—the very damn loveliest imported best!*

She climbed into the tub and, sinking beneath the warm scented water, allowed herself to drift upon a sea of imagination in which all the splendor of the world became her very own. . . .

It was just after nine. The maid had arrived, had called her in sick and was now occupied with the disorder of the kitchen.

Marian was dressed and seated at the desk in the living room. She was writing a series of checks made out to a liquor store, two supermarkets, a Proctor drugstore, a dress shop and a department store. The checks amounted to four hundred dollars, eighty above what was needed to pay Killian. She would bet the eighty dollars with the bartender, since Killian had stopped her credit permanently.

It would take time to cash the checks, and the odds against being able to meet them were great. Though Warren would naturally make good before he would allow her to be prosecuted, she saw him as the single cause of her trouble and she was seething with resentment. She was also nervous, chain-smoking and sipping a martini. She was writing the last check when the phone rang.

"Marian?"

"Yes, speaking."

"Marian Ostermann?"

That was her maiden name. No one ever used it! "Who is this?"

"It's Tony." Chuckle. "Surprise, huh?"

"Tony? Tony who?"

"Tony who else? Tony Viani." Chuckle. "How many Tonys you know, Marian?"

She held the phone dumbly, unable to speak. Tony Viani! It must be—how long?—three years. She had said good-bye to him at the door one night and the next day he had vanished without a trace. Six months later she married Warren.

"Tony," she said. "My God, Tony, Tony! Whatever happened to you?"

"It was getting too hot for me in Miami. And I don't mean the weather. I took off."

"Well, all right, Tony. But you could have called me! Oh, God—you did owe me that much."

"Marian—listen! I had a wife. And a kid. Out in L. A. I went back to them, for a time. Then I got a divorce. I'm free now."

"Sure, fine. But *I'm* not! And you never told me you were married."

"There were a lot of things I never told you, kiddo. Sometimes it's the best way."

18

"I don't agree, Tony. I don't agree at all."

"Still betting the nags, Marian?"

"That's just like you, Tony. Change the subject when it's going against you."

"That was always your pet subject, baby. Horses. Remember?"

How could she forget? During that time just before Tony, she was twelve-hundred-fifty dollars in the red to a book in Miami and couldn't pay, as usual.

The man came for her one night just as she was getting dressed for a date. He told her Mr. Viani wanted to see her about the gambling debt and Mr. Viani never took "no" for an answer. There was a quiet aura of menace about the man which convinced her she had better not argue. So she went along with him.

In silence Tony had stared at her from behind his desk for what seemed close to a full minute. She had never seen such eyes anywhere in the soft world of her experience. They were savage, violent and nakedly evil. They were also sensual woman-wise and hypnotic as the unblinking gaze of a reptile. She was fascinated, but terribly frightened.

Suddenly he smiled and the whole texture of his personality changed.

"C'mon," he said. "We'll go to dinner and we'll talk about it. I got a hunch I may be able to get you off the hook."

She went to bed with him that first night. Not out of fear. She wanted to. She had to! He was like a jungle animal who understood no law but the law of superior advantage and brute force. He was the only man who could dominate the untamed part of herself which laughed disdainfully at the weak males who sooner or later laid their silly egos and their groveling hungers at her feet. He was the first real

19

challenge, and she had to have the unbridled power of him writhing in her bed.

He was a superb lover as it turned out. And, surprisingly, for all his savage hungers, he was often gentle.

In the most irrevocable sense, for perhaps the first time in her life, she fell in love. And she meekly dedicated her entire devotion to Tony, while he gave nothing of himself to her but the superficial cries of passion. He still remained a mystery and a challenge, and this was the key to her surrender for she soon grew bored with anyone who danced at her command.

In the morning Tony canceled her debt, moved her into a regal hotel-apartment at the beach and made her his mistress.

She knew he was a power in charge of a segment of Miami gambling interests and guessed that he was involved in other, more dangerous activities. But he told her little and made it plain that she was an outsider so far as his "business" was concerned. He provided much, she loved him much and didn't care. She more than loved hm, she was his total slave.

She hinted at marriage but he was always evasive. "Aw," he might say, "marriage would ruin it for us, baby. If we really *had* to live together we'd be at each other's throats in a couple of days. Hold on awhile. I got a lot of problems to settle first. One day I'll retire from this racket and then we'll see."

Instead, he simply vanished. And no one would admit, if they knew, where he had gone. So she waited a couple of months and when he didn't show, didn't even phone or write, she moved to New York. She got the job with Proctor, and in his office she met Warren when he came one day to discuss the stock investments of her boss.

She married Warren in a mood composed of rebellion and defeat. He was a lot of man, he had looks and money and he was the best substitute for the aching loss of Tony she could find.

Now she was angry with Tony. Did he think he could come barging in three years later and pick up where he left off?

"Tony," she cried. "Let's skip the chit-chat. I'm on my way out and I'm in a hurry. What do you want?"

"You," he said bluntly.

"Uh-uh, Tony, not me. Never. I'm married, I love my husband and I'm going to stay married. Did you think nothing would change in three years? It's too late, Tony."

"I'm at the Roosevelt Hotel," he answered. "Room Fourteen twenty-two. I'll wait one hour."

"Tony! Didn't you hear me say I was married? You can wait one hour or a hundred, I won't be there. How did you find me, anyway?"

"Easy. One of your girl friends in Miami. So this guy you're married to, you got a big thing for him, huh?" His voice sounded detached, a little bored.

"I'm mad about him, Tony. Simply mad about him!"

"Yeah," he said. "Well, have a good, square life, Marian. See you around."

*Click!* And he was gone.

Marian looked at the phone in amazement. Oh, damn! The smug gall of that man! She drummed her fingers on the desk. Why didn't I tell him I don't care about Warren at all? Right this minute I could strangle him!

She got the hotel number from information, quickly dialed it and demanded 1422.

"Yeah?"

"Tony, listen. I—you didn't even give me a chance to say good-bye. Besides, I have a favor I want to ask you."

"Sure, Marian. How much?"

"Oh, Tony, for heaven's sake!"

"How much?"

"About five hundred. I bet myself into a hole, and I'm a little short this week."

"C'mon over and we'll talk about it. One hour. Don't keep me waiting, I'm not here for laughs. I got a lotta business to handle."

He hung up.

Marian took the little pile of checks she had been writing and, smiling slyly, tore them into tiny fragments. She dropped the pieces into the wastebasket.

Now she moved to the wall mirror and studied herself carefully. With her finger she made a final adjustment to her lipstick.

She turned abruptly and crossed to the desk. She found paper and scrawled a note.

Warren,
    Went to the city to visit a girl friend. I won't be home until late. There's a steak in the refrig.
    Have fun!

                        Marian

She read the note and decided it was exactly right for him, but it was bad judgment. Better cover the retreat in case things didn't work out with Tony. She tore up the note and started again.

Darling,
    Went to the city to meet an old girl friend from out of town. I may get stuck for dinner and a show. Ugh! But I'll call if I'm going to be late.
    Forgive me for being such an awful bitch this morn-

22

ing. Didn't mean a word and I'm going to reform. You'll see!

Love you,
Marian

There! Play it smart and have your little revenge in secret—eh, Marian?

A picture flashed across the screen of her mind. Tony was framed in the doorway to the hotel room, eyeing her with unconcealed lust.

She entered. Tony kissed her, almost brutally, his hand wandering from her breasts downward, sneaking under her dress, exploring between her legs.

*Ahhh. Ahhh, Tony, Tony! Don't hurry, darling. Let's make it a ritual, an all-day production . . .*

Still smiling slightly, her face a study in trancelike sensuality, she went to speak with the maid.

Then she hurried to the hall closet to get her very best coat and hat.

23

# — THREE —

WARREN EMRICK WAS ABOUT AS STONED as he could get on a commercial airliner without drawing attention to himself.

During the entire flight he had been sipping "coffee" from a thermos. "Always carry my own coffee, Miss." He didn't mention that the coffee was laced with bourbon in a ratio of about five to one.

And he couldn't mention that he was a little drunk because he came home one night and found his wife had fled, taking with her nearly every dime he had in the world.

His senses were not really dulled. If anything they had become sharper. The alcohol was eating away the last thread of restraint which held his anger, allowing him to concentrate upon it with a kind of perverse joy, freeing him to conjure up the most insidious, the most uncivilized plans of vengeance.

He had taken a month's leave of absence and, if necessary, he would take two or three more—six months, a year if need be, even if it cost him his job!

"Sir! Won't you *please* fasten your seat belt!" She had to tell him twice—because now the jet was close to setting down over the neon blaze of Miami, the city having appeared so suddenly after the dark blanket of ocean that it seemed a gaudy mirage in the desert of night.

Fumbling with the belt, he looked up into the precise bitter-sweet face of the stewardess, hating the tidy uniform and the jaunty cap perched above that little knife-blade of mechanical smile.

"Sorry, honey," he cracked. "I wouldn't want to spoil your whole goddamm night!" *Cocky bitch!* he said without sound to her retreating back.

The plane banked steeply, aiming a wing tip at some car-strewn artery in the sparkling crazy-quilt below. And he thought, *I know you're down there, Marian. Boozing in one of those lighted sewers, or writhing in some dark slimy cave.*

*And I'm going to find you. I'm going to hunt you until I find you, Marian. That's a promise, you sneaky bitch!* His hands worked against each other, squeezing, squeezing, the memory of her soft slender neck. . .

Some six weeks following the day she went to the city to visit "an old girl friend from out of town," Warren had come home from the office to find the apartment gutted of all her possessions. In fact, practically everything of value was gone, including some of those articles which he considered exclusively his own—an expensive camera, a two-hundred-dollar pair of binoculars, a fine hunting rifle (my God, a hunting rifle!), a portable typewriter and a perpetual-movement clock.

Somehow the removal of those personal items which he brought to the marriage doubled his fury. To find that his wife was not only a thief but a petty thief damaged her image beyond repair.

During the six weeks before she disappeared, Marian had won his absolute pardon, his total forgiveness. She had returned the money she had "borrowed" from him and apparently she had kept her promise to give up betting the horses, an absurdly childish compulsion which he could never quite understand. If Marian had just about everything money could buy (excluding the luxuries of the rich) what was the gain in trying to win a few extra dollars on the ponies? Forgetting taxes, with salary and allowance, she had a hundred seventy-five a week pure spending money! How many wives could say the same? Furthermore, she held the job on her own whim, for her own selfish extras, and could have lounged around the apartment all day doing nothing if she so desired.

In any case, for a time she had been a model wife. She was good-humored even when he was unreasonable, or irritable, she was affectionate and companionable, she was an unfailingly enthusiastic bed-partner.

The moody silences she used to indulge were a thing of the past. She told him amusing tales of her days at the office. And she kept him posted on the not so amusing details of the weird extortion plot which had just recently cost Proctor Drugs a quarter of a million dollars.

Looking back, she seemed strangely alive and spirited, caught up by some excitement which could not be justified by any visible change in the basic structure of her life.

She made his favorite drinks and fixed those special meals which pleased him. She was attentive and thoughtful, forgetting none of those little comforts which made him want to rush away from the tiresome manipulations of the stock market to that five-room island of joy in Jackson Heights.

In short—the horrible bitch was setting him up for the kill!

It happened on a morning when he was placed completely off guard, lulled to sleep by this continuous barrage of good deeds and good will. Anything so temporary as a single night or even three days of sweetness and light would have caused him to seriously doubt her and so watch for the trap. But six weeks of uncompromising devotion, without a hint that she sought some reward, made it appear to him that she had indeed reformed as promised, had really altered certain elements of her character which were distasteful.

On that morning, luck played on her side. Or was it that she kept him in bed too long with teasing delays, artful caresses and exotic inventiveness? Probably. Yes, very likely the latter! Anyway, he was late, unusually late. And when she tricked him with that casual remark about the rent and the need to transfer funds to checking, he had one foot out the door. . .

"Oh, wait a minute, dear! Did you know that the rent is due, along with all the other monthly bills?"

"So?"

"So I just made out the checks for you to sign yesterday and there wasn't enough money in your checking account to cover. I have the morning off—do you want me to run down to the bank and transfer from savings?"

"Damn! I wish you'd told me earlier, honey. I'm already late for an appointment and I don't have time to fool with it."

"Well, darling, all you have to do is sign the withdrawal slip and I'll take care of the rest."

"Okay, okay. Go get it!"

She came back with a blank savings check, a book to support it and a pen. Quickly he signed on the top of the two signature lines and immediately she withdrew book and check, saying, "We're a hundred sixty short—how much should I fill this out for?"

In the past he had always filled in the amount himself, even if she made the transfer. But now there seemed such complete harmony and trust between them it would be insulting to demand the check back so that he could write the figures himself. Besides, he was in such a hurry and she was only trying to be helpful.

27

"Make it five hundred," he said. Then he kissed her and raced down the hall for the elevator.

Of course that was a fatal mistake—because when he came home that night to find her gone, he got the bank book and discovered she had taken forty-seven of the forty-eight thousand dollars in the account, leaving him all but broke.

Everything gone—his money, his personal things (What would she do with a rifle?), her clothes and other belongings, and finally she herself had vanished without so much as a note left behind her.

There was a time of weeping and utter desolation. But it didn't last long, was soon replaced by the most violent anger. And now he began a relentless search for her, rushing to the office of his lawyer.

"I'm sorry, Warren," the lawyer told him with a solemn shake of the head, "unless you can find her, and fast, there's very little I could do. Morally speaking, she's a thief and a fraud, I agree. But legally—well, that's another matter. The money was jointly held and your signature gave her the right to even that part which was yours. How are you going to prove fraud? You don't have a single witness.

"Now we could get a court order to stop her from spending that money until a judge determined just how it was to be divided. And I feel quite certain that in a divorce settlement you would come out with at least half of it, since the largest part of the money was earned by you before the marriage. But first you'd have to find her. And obviously the money would have to be intact. You can't divide funds that no longer exist.

"So I'd suggest you hire private detectives and run her down in a hurry. Sorry, but I'm afraid that's the only hope I have to offer you, old man. . ."

And that was no hope at all. Private detectives!

At better than a hundred a day? Impossible! He'd find her himself.

Of one thing he was certain. There was a man in the picture, standing in the background cheering her on. Marian was not one to hustle off into the night without the strong arms of a man around her, forty-seven thousand dollars notwithstanding. And likely the man had been some down-on-his-luck sharpie who damn well helped her plot how to take him before they ran!

Where would she meet such a character? At the office? Hardly. How about one of the race track set —some contact she made while betting the horses? That's closer, that's more logical.

Someone out of her past? But who? For the very reason that he was a jealous sort, she had been vague about her male friends in that life before they met. But she was practically a stranger in New York when he found her and therefore it was ten to one that if she was involved with a man from the past, he would be out of Miami.

It was a tense, exhausting period of trial and error, of footwork, phone calls, questions, questions. All fruitless. By not so much as a chance remark to any-one had she given herself away.

Finally, through Proctor Drugs (they were not exactly pleased with her since she left without no-tice), he got the name of her former employer in Miami. She must have told him but he had long ago forgotten, knowing only that it was some title com-pany having to do with things like abstracts and escrows and title insurance.

Burkholtz Title & Abstract Company. That was it! She had been secretary to a vice-president. But when he called, they told him the man had died a few months before. Well, was there anyone else in the firm who knew her? Perhaps one of the other secretaries or office workers.

There had been a letter from some girl in Miami (he never did know her name), and Warren felt there was a slim hope that if he could find this girl she might know something.

They connected him with a Miss Zimmerman. Yes, she remembered Marian well. No, she hadn't been in touch with her for years, not since Marian left for New York. Anyone else? Well, there was Anita Wymer, formerly Marian's best friend. But Miss Wymer had moved her talents to the executive offices of a supermarket chain. Would he like the number?

Miss Wymer was most pleasant. Somehow, too pleasant, too stridently earnest. Marian? Of course, of course! But no, not a *thing* since her last letter a couple of months ago—just chit-chat, you understand. Was there a hint that she might be visiting Miami soon? No, not one single word! If Anita Wymer had the slightest notion that Marian was coming she would have rolled out the red carpet long ago!

Did Miss Wymer know any of Marian's old boy friends? Well, not really. They had double-dated, of course. But that was long ago and she had forgotten even the names of those people. They had all become lost in the shuffle and now Miss Wymer had a whole new set of friends. Besides, she thought Marian was married to a very important man in New York and *divinely* happy. What made Mr. Bradford (this was the name Warren gave her) think he could locate her through people in Miami when she was certainly still in New York?

Warren said he had gone to see Mr. Emrick and Marian's husband said they were now separated and he did not know where she was. So he, Mr. Bradford, thought maybe he could locate her in Miami. It was most important because though he did not know

Marian personally, he wanted her to testify in a legal matter involving a title which had been searched by her ex-boss, now dead. He was perfectly willing to see that she was well paid for her trouble.

Miss Wymer was extremely, sincerely sorry, but she still did not know where Marian Emrick could be located.

Period! But Warren did not believe this was so. Anita Wymer had been just too damn positive, too gushingly, sincerely perplexed. She protested her innocence too much and with too many nervous adjectives. Furthermore, some of her little speech sounded rehearsed. He could hear the voice of Marian behind Wymer's pitch. . .

"Anita, listen! No matter *who* calls, I don't care if it's the Governor of New York, you don't know where I am. You don't know a *thing* about me! . . ."

Warren was pretty damn sure that Wymer knew where he could find Marian, and if he had to scare her into a confession or break her arm, any way at all, he was going to make her talk! In any event, he might pick up other clues from other sources and the flight to Miami would not be wasted.

The jet sank to the runway with a grunt of tires and began to taxi toward the bright cluster of terminals.

A marriage and a career shot to hell, thought Warren. Love and money—gone! The hell with love, give me the money! Man's best friend. His only friend!

Forty-seven thousand! The sum total of a whole career. Years of tireless research and calculation; of watching and waiting and speculating and sweating against the odds. A hundred-million words of advice to arrogant or whining customers. A hundred-million miles of ticker tape unwinding the idiot fractions, the spastic fluctuations, before the aching shuttling eyeballs.

31

When she stole the money, Marian simply poured those grinding interminable years down the drain. The forty-seven thousands were symbols of achievement, the rewards of effort, the prizes of victory.

And without these green symbols, in effect, a man was nothing. He was a beggar in an indifferent world. He was a slinking shadow without a voice in all the markets of commerce where the symbols commanded respect and attention.

He thought, You don't make a man nothing, Marian. You don't make a joke of his whole life and get away with it, sister. You've got trouble, baby. Hard on your little round heels. You and lover-boy, whoever he is.

*I could mangle them. I could kill them both and sleep like a wino in an alley—not a single regret!*

You thought you were just an ordinary human being with average inclinations, all mild enough. You were often selfish, sometimes jealous, occasionally resentful and, in rare moments, downright angry—though you still behaved in a civilized manner.

But you were also thoughtful, compassionate, generous. You bought people presents and you spared their feelings and you were polite and had a sense of humor and sometimes you wanted to weep over all the individual calamities you saw around you.

Then—suddenly—you were a savage! You were not just angry, you were in a rage of hate. You were a man with a loaded gun in his pocket and you were going out there into that neon jungle to hunt—and to kill! Kill with the insane joy of a maniac.

And the need of vengeance was so terrible that if you didn't have it soon you might turn against the first person who crossed you with a careless word and beat his face into a splintered mass of broken bones with your bare hands.

They were leaving the plane now, moving down

the stairs. The man in front was wise-cracking over his shoulder to the stewardess, delaying Warren's progress, while the thing exploded inside him.

"Hey, Romeo!" he said. "Why don't you shut your face and get out of my way!"

He gave the man a shove that sent him nearly sprawling. Saved by his grip on the railing, the man turned, his anger replaced by fear at what he saw in Warren's face.

"What—what's the matter with you?" the man said weakly. "You must be out of your mind!"

Knowing it was true, Warren pushed past him and hurled himself down the stairs, into the terminal.

# – FOUR –

Anita Wymer lived in Miami Beach. Her apartment was in a small, white-stucco building fronting the bay.

Warren found the address in the telephone book and, since he was not a stranger to Miami, he simply rented a car at the airport and drove to Wymer's place as fast as he could push the Chevy through the considerable traffic of early evening.

He climbed a flight of stairs, searched down a hall and knocked on a door. It opened.

"Miss Wymer? Anita Wymer?"

"Yes."

"I'm Bradford, Dave Bradford. I talked with you on the phone yesterday from New York."

"Oh," she said. "Yes, I remember. But I hope you didn't make the trip just to see me. Because I told you everything I know."

Miss Wymer was a honey-blonde in her late twenties, one of the few remaining whose long hair had not been victimized by the sheers of some local beauty butcher. She had small delicate features and crisp purposeful blue eyes. A rich café-au-lait tan and a stunning figure made her altogether quite a package. But Warren hardly noticed.

"No," he replied. "I didn't make the trip just to see you. I have other business. But as long as I'm here—"

"Mr. Bradford, really, you're just wasting your time. If I knew where you could find Marian I'd be glad to tell you. There would be no point in keeping it a secret."

Neither her looks nor her attitude matched her phone personality. She seemed cool and formidable. Warren knew it was possible that she had been fortified by Marian since he had spoken to her long distance.

"Look," he said determinedly, "you might have some clue which would help me locate this woman. Just a few questions, that's all. May I come in?"

"I'm sorry, no. I was just going out."

Warren made a show of taking in the casual sun dress, the straw sandals. He could barely resist the urge to shove her backward into the room.

Their eyes locked.

She shrugged. "All right," she said, standing aside and letting him pass. "But just for a minute. I have some important matters to attend to this evening."

"I'll bet," cracked Warren as she closed the door.

"Mr. Bradford," she snapped, "I'm not sure I like your attitude! You sound hostile to me."

"Do I?" Warren glanced around him. He stood in a small, immaculate living room containing modern pieces done in harmonic graduating shades of basic blue composition—lavender, turquoise, magenta. It was quite effective. The typical picture window framed a view of the bay.

Warren sat down, crossed his legs, lighted a cigarette and leaned back in the manner of a visitor preparing himself for a long stay.

Miss Wymer, sitting precariously on the edge of a chair, was quick to notice. Tight lines of irritation pulled sharply at her features.

"Now what is it you want to know?" she said bitingly.

"I want to know why you're lying to me about Marian Emrick," Warren said flatly.

"You listen here, Mr. whatever-your-name-is, I

35

don't have to stand for that kind of talk in my own home!"

"No, but you will for Marian's sake," said Warren. "If you knew her better—if you *really* knew her—you wouldn't waste a minute protecting her. Or would you?"

Miss Wymer sat very still. She studied him with cool unblinking eyes. "You're the husband, aren't you? You're Warren Emrick."

Warren returned her gaze. "That's right. I'm the husband. And I'm not leaving until you tell me where to find her. Just make up your mind to that and you'll save yourself a lot of trouble."

"If Marian left you, she had a good reason. I'm beginning to understand that reason. You're not exactly the lovable type. Still, I suppose you must care a lot for her or you wouldn't race across the country after her."

"Miss Wymer, if you plucked a beautiful branch from a tree and it turned out to be a deadly snake, you'd know how I feel about Marian. I hate the evil bitch! What I *do* care for is the forty-seven thousand bucks she stole from me before she sneaked off. I intend to get that dough back. And anyone who stands in my way is going to get hurt."

"Does that include me?"

He nodded. "You bet it does, honey. The frailty of the female sex no longer brings a tear to my eye. It makes me laugh out loud to think how helpless you women are. So, honey, your best defense is to just tell me where to find that slut and my money. I want to be friendly, so I'll give you thirty seconds."

Miss Wymer lighted a cigarette, shifted nervously in her chair. "Marian once told me that she inherited some money and that she put this money in a joint account with you. So I imagine she just took what was hers when she left."

36

Warren laughed without mirth. "The only thing Marian ever inherited in her whole life was a sick mind. Yeah, and a hatful of losing tickets on the ponies. Marian is a thief and a liar. And if you're her best friend, what are you?"

"All right, that's enough! I'm going to—"

"You're going to tell me where to find her, that's what you're going to do, sister! If Marian made up some story about inheriting money, she made it up *after* she ran with mine. You just gave yourself away. Naturally she had to explain her sudden wealth to her old friend, Anita."

He stood, then moved toward her. "Where is she?" he shouted.

"I suppose you're going to use force now," Anita Wymer said defiantly, though she rose from her chair and backed toward the door. Fear was in her eyes and flight in the tense coil of her body.

Warren hated her. He saw her as Marian's friend and therefore an accomplice, an enemy. He sprang forward and caught her by the hair. He lifted his open hand to smash it across her face.

The phone rang.

"Answer it," said Warren, releasing her. "And watch what you say. I'll be listening."

She moved into a bedroom. He followed. The phone was on a night table. She caught up the receiver, but he grabbed it from her and held it so they could both listen.

"Anita?"

"This is Anita."

"It's Tony. We're over in Miami, on the town. We're gonna do it big, top to bottom. Wanna join us? I got a guy for you, a real swinger. I'll send him to pick you up. Half an hour—okay?"

It was a heavy voice, demanding, arrogant. Warren

37

lost interest. He had thought it might be Marian by some sweet quirk of fate.

"I'd like to, Tony. But I just can't tonight. I have a date."

"Okay. So bring 'im along."

"Can't do that either, Tony. We're going to a party. I'd invite you but I don't know the people. Listen, I'll call you in the morning, all right?"

"Sure, kid. Don't forget. Marian will—"

"Good-bye, Tony."

She hung up.

Warren stared at her. "Marian will what, Anita?"

"He was talking about a different Marian," she said quickly. "My God, the world is full of Marians!"

"Sure. But it happens this one stole my money. Okay, Anita, I've had it. Up to here! I'm fresh out of patience. I'll just take this whole place apart until I find Marian's address. And if that doesn't work, you'll come apart next."

He pushed her ahead of him into the living room. He crossed to a limed-oak desk.

"I'm going to call the police," she threatened.

"You just do that. I hope you do. They'll put your friend Marian away for about ten years. They're already hunting for her in New York," he bluffed. "Go right ahead. You might get a couple of years yourself as an accessory after the fact."

He watched her closely, saw doubt and fear shadow her face. "Logically," he said, "the best place to start would be here at this desk." He began to open drawers, pulling them out, emptying the contents on the desk top.

"Never mind," she said wearily. "Bottom right-hand drawer. An address book with a green cover."

He found the book and began to thumb through it.

"Under her maiden name," said Anita.

Warren had to reach back in his mind. He had almost forgotten, so seldom was the name mentioned.

He flipped the pages until he came to Ostermann. There were several scratch-outs, then an address on Biscayne Key and a phone number. He copied them down.

At the door she asked, "Was that really *your* money Marian took?"

"Yes, my money."

"I don't believe you."

"And I couldn't care less. Tell me about this bastard, Tony. Who is he?"

"You'll have to find out for yourself."

"Ahh, loyalty. Well, I have plans for Tony."

"Would you really have hurt me?"

"Yes. But later I might have been sorry. Though I'm not even sure of that."

He opened the door and went out.

# – FIVE –

It was a lemon-colored, one-story house a block from the bay on Biscayne Key. The house was dark but Warren rang the bell anyway.

After a minute of listening he went around back. There was the usual screened porch called a Florida Room. It had jalousie windows and a door opening upon a patio. The door was wood frame with glass louvers protecting a screen.

He had to break one of the glass sections in order to poke a hole in the screen and unlock the door. He entered, groped for a wall switch and brazenly turned on the lights. As he went from room to room he turned on other lights.

He didn't care about the lights. He didn't care if he was seen or not. His anger was too big for creeping and cringing in darkness. His conviction that all his acts were justified by the treachery of his wife was enormous, his reasoning twisted out of shape in the heat of his fury.

He could do no wrong. He was the self-appointed policeman, jury and executioner.

The interior of the house tried to appear luxurious and expensively furnished. But to a critical eye it was merely gaudy, the flashy pieces in bad taste and of cheap construction. Warren guessed that the house was rented. Now, in the winter season, it could bring a thousand a month.

There were three bedrooms, each with a bath. Warren stormed through them, opening closets, yanking at bureau drawers in search of the money.

There was only men's clothing in the two smaller rooms. But then he came upon a third which might have been described by a fatuous real estate agent as the master bedroom.

Here there were twin closets. One was locked. The other contained the abundance of Marian's wardrobe—the expensive suits, dresses, cocktail and evening gowns his money had bought her.

He began to examine the dresses one by one, remembering some occasion on which each was worn, his face terrible with hate and sorrow. After a time he took one of the dresses and tore it savagely, ripped it into useless shreds. He went down the rack, lifting out other dresses and mutilating them with demented energy.

Tiring of this he returned to his search for the money. There must be at least a bank book, a deposit box key, a receipt. But where?

He examined the lock on the other closet. It appeared a simple latch type, not much of a problem for anyone with a little skill and determination.

He returned from the kitchen with a screw driver and a knife. Working them together he was able to move the latch out of the slot, prying it back until the door opened.

The closet was stocked with costly suits and sport jackets, also shirts, ties and a dozen or more pairs of shoes, all top quality. On a shelf above these items there was an assortment of hand guns which included three automatics and four revolvers. In wall brackets were a shotgun and a hunting rifle—his own!

On the floor of the closet he found his portable typewriter and, beside it a tan suitcase of the airplane luggage variety, strong but lightweight. He hoisted this onto the bed and opened it.

The money was there! In fact there was nothing else in the case but green bundles of currency. Perhaps *more* than forty-seven thousand, a great deal more!

He decided to count it. Because the bills were large and the currency bundled in labeled stacks, the count was swift. It came to an even two hundred forty-five thousand, nearly a quarter of a million dollars!

Smiling grimly he put the money away, closed the case and sat down to think. With so many guns about and what could be the clothing of a small nest of hoods, it seemed obvious that this Tony was not exactly a legitimate businessman. Knowing Marian, Tony was probably on the winning side of the gambling racket and the quarter million was the take from some giant bookie operation.

If Tony came home from his night on the town with Marian and found the loot gone he might run howling in many directions. But it was unlikely that the police department would hear so much as a whisper of complaint from him. And that was good. It was even funny. The dice were fixed in Warren's favor.

He went back to the closet and removed the pistols from the shelf. Every gun was fully loaded and seemed, if not new, in perfect condition. His own .38 was in his pocket and Warren did not need or want the weapons. But why leave such an arsenal in the hands of an outraged punk?

He opened the case and placed the pistols, along with his own dismantled rifle, beside the money. To this store he added several boxes of ammunition which he also spied in the closet. Tony could have the shotgun. The suitcase was already overloaded.

Now he got the portable typewriter and carried it to a desk in the living room. For a moment he searched the desk, coming up with only one item of interest—a phone bill addressed to one Tony Viani.

There was also paper in the desk and, inserting a sheet, he began to peck laboriously.

Dear Lover-boy Tony,

I'm going to tear up your IOU, Tony. If you're a nice boy I might even let you off with your life.

I acknowledge payment for the following:

1. Cash stolen from my bank account with the aid of dear, dear Marian—$47,000.

2. The theft of one slightly soiled, slightly used wife, including settlement for expenses, time, mental anguish and other intangibles suffered when the treacherous bitch ran off with you to this YMCA of crime, this sweaty sewer of love. Cost to you—$198,000. Is she worth it, Tony?

Strangely, the grand total comes to exactly $245,000.

You got off easy, Tony boy. If you had been here I would have killed you—slowly, very, very slowly, Tony. Remember that, and don't push your luck.

As for you, Marian—I'll think about it. I may just break a few bones or throw acid in your face. Something mild like that, in view of my joy over this wealth you brought me. In any case, I'll be seeing you, baby.

Good-bye, dear friends. Your generosity overwhelms me. It moves me to tears.

Be brave. Keep chuckling.

W. E.

Warren fastened the note to the closet door with a piece of Scotch Tape from the desk. Carrying the suitcase and his typewriter, he went out the front way, leaving the house in a glorious blaze of lights.

He stowed the case and the typewriter in the trunk and drove off merrily. The grin kept widening across his face. He began to laugh. He couldn't stop. He would grow silent for a space, but then every few blocks the beautiful irony of it all would strike him and the sound would come bubbling from deep inside him.

It was just an investment, he thought. You put forty-seven thousand in the capable hands of Marian

43

and Tony and practically overnight it became a quarter million.

He braked before one of the swank, towering beach hotels.

*Ahh, Marian, ahh, Tony, how I love you both! How clever you are, how brilliant. How wisely you increase my capital. How generously you pay for your little mistakes.*

The bellhop had the two suitcases in hand.

"Be careful of that one, my boy," Warren said grandly, pointing to the tan case. It's simply stuffed with money. I always bring one case full of clothes and another full of money!"

He had to laugh again, knowing he would not be taken seriously. At first the bellhop's face was blank. But suddenly he smiled and began to chuckle in a kind of echo of Warren's deep rumble.

They moved off into the lobby.

# — SIX —

TONY VIANI WAS ENJOYING THE SHOW. His thick, brooding features, rock-ribbed and intense as a cocked gun, were clenched in a lewd grin.

On the raised platform, square and ugly as a boxing ring, the girl rotated her bottom, twirled her naked breasts, pumped her groin and writhed about the stage to the thumping bleating sounds of musical bedlam. The girl was young and, even for a stripper, vastly endowed with a fleshy sensuality that reached across the footlights in nearly visible waves of magnetism.

Marian, who sat ringside with Tony and a slim hollow-cheeked man who had a long narrow face and hair the color of wet sand, did not watch the stripper. Instead, her gaze was fastened upon Tony, her expression at once speculative and adoring. The stripper was a bore, but Tony's reaction to her lusty contortions was a matter of high interest, especially since this same stripper had been at their table between gyrations—invited by Tony to make it a foursome. And though this babe was supposed to be paired with Tony's friend, Earl Lubeck, she had tossed words, eyes and curves at Tony in the most obvious play for his attention.

You could not really tell with any certainty what Tony was thinking. His expression boldly described pleasure or displeasure. But in between these extremes his face was a mask, an enigma. Nor did his words very often signal his actions. So without warning he might be taken by some shocking whim and would trample anyone just to follow the sudden impulse to amuse or benefit himself.

For instance, if Tony got even a small itch for this teaser, this Sheila La Belle, he would think nothing at all of going off somewhere with her when she finished her last grind. Marian would be left in the hands of Earl Lubeck until Tony returned without so much as a grunt of apology.

And no plea of threat could reach him. You could take him or leave him, that's all. Tony held all the cards because he cared so little about anyone else but himself. If you didn't like his ruthless ways you could depart immediately and he would feel no pain, no pang of regret.

Tony was important to women. But women were not important to Tony.

It was this very quality which fascinated Marian. Tony would always be a challenge. And she would always hope to break him down. Though if that doubtful day ever came, she would promptly lose interest.

But for the moment Marian was not really worried about Sheila La Belle. Tony was just treading water for an hour or two. Tony had plans—the most awesome plans—to be carried out before the night would end. And these plans could never include Sheila.

The so-called music died with an agonized squeal. Sheila jiggled, bounced and bowed her way offstage, hugging her giant breasts from view as her native modesty returned in the harsh glare of a naked spotlight.

So facile were her costume changes, she appeared at the table in only a minute, dressed in a purple gown boasting her cleavage. She gave Earl a playful nudge with her elbow, winked moltenly at Tony and offered Marian a shy tentative smile of truce—which

46

was like hoisting a white flag in the face of a snarling leopard.

Tony, his arm around Marian, leered at Sheila and ordered more champagne.

Meanwhile, the M.C. had loped onstage from the wings and had begun a graceless burlesque of Miss La Belle's strip performance. Soon he had peeled down to his shorts. He was a tall, narrow-chested, paunchy man, his sickly pale skin beading sweat under the lights as he wound his rump grotesquely.

Marian turned away in disgust but Tony, who had a very basic sense of humor, clapped his hands and made growling sounds of approval.

Now, in the semigloom, a shadow appeared at the table. Turning slowly, Tony looked up into the man's eyes. Glee fled from Tony's face, replaced by a hard look of cunning perception. Tony barely nodded and the man vanished.

Tony signaled the waitress and, with merely a glance at the check, returned it with a hundred-dollar bill.

"You're not leaving, are you?" asked Sheila of Tony with a quizzical lift of her winged, pencil-smeared eyebrows. "Why honey you—" She glanced around her—"you guys will miss my last show. It's the best, the way-out best!" Her false lashes fluttered her false despair.

"Don't cry," said Tony. "You'll wake the customers." He plucked a fifty from a great fist of bills and tucked it between her breasts. "Right in the bank, baby. Keep it open. I might be back with another deposit."

"Anytime," said Sheila, with a wide money-grin. "You know my combination, honey."

Marian gave Tony a scorching look, but he was oblivious to it. His face had closed. Without waiting

47

for Marian or Lubeck, he stood and moved away toward the door.

Outside, as Tony appeared on the walk, headlights flared and a dark-blue Cadillac sedan whispered to the curb. Tony moved lightly toward it, though he was a big man with massive shoulders and the sinewy hawser-thick biceps of certain day laborers. Indeed, his father had been the foreman of a sandhog crew. And Tony had, for a space in his twenties, worked under the old man as a driller with tireless energy and a kind of surly obedience.

It was a tough, man-crushing job and Tony had seen many a mucker or driller die, sealed in a watery tomb of his own making. During this period Tony had formed the callus of body and soul which provided a nearly unbreakable shell against physical and emotional pain.

But Tony had grown up. He had seen that the take came not to the workers who built the tunnels in the agony of endless toil and danger, but to the city registers in the little booths outside the tunnels where, day and night, the clinking coins sang an endless chorus as they were swallowed in the maw of civil profit.

There was a parallel which Tony observed. People everywhere in their grubby little jobs were the suckers who sold themselves for peanuts while their employers fattened and grew rich—likewise the race tracks and their stockholders, the bookies, the casino operators, the syndicates and their bosses. All the crooks of the world minted a huge and certain profit while trampling under foot that debris of humanity called the "little people."

And so Tony grew to be strong and cruel. He decided he would be one of the guys who stood laughing at the tunnel gates of the world, collecting his tolls.

Now Tony opened the rear door of the sedan and climbed in. Marian, who had just then stepped from the night club with Lubeck, took her seat beside him. Lubeck closed the door and hopped in front beside the driver, Harry Rosen, the shadow whose silent appearance at their table had sparked their departure.

Rosen steered the big car north along Biscayne Boulevard, pressing the buttons that closed the electric windows as he turned on the air conditioner. The Cadillac was new and purred smoothly, weaving neatly around slower vehicles under Rosen's skillful guidance.

"Not so fast, Harry." Tony's voice, the voice of all true leaders—soft, withstrained, in command, merely hinting at deep reserves of inner strength and complex power. "There's plenty of time." He glanced at his watch to confirm. "We don't want to offend the police, do we, Harry?"

Rosen chuckled, slackened speed. "Well, I'll tell ya, Tony. I got a clean record. I wouldn't want the cops to have anything on me like a traffic violation."

They all laughed, all except Marian who pulled nervously on a cigarette, her face drawn with anxiety

Silence again closed around them, as if that small bantering exchange of words had been only a flimsy screen to hide the truth of the inevitable which lay ahead.

Rosen braked for a signal, found a cigarette and punched the dash lighter. He drew smoke in deeply and exhaled with a long sigh as he flipped the indicator for the turn and wheeled west on the green light.

He was a chunky man with a round, deceptively

mild face. His rusty-brown hair was abundant, though receding in a widow's peak. He had a sharp nose and heavy lips. He smiled frequently and in a way which gave him a look of boyish innocence.

He may once have been a boy, but innocent— never. He had been a scrappy troublemaker from the day he put away his roller skates in favor of a zip gun. He was a reform-school graduate who had once worked side by side with Tony, tunneling beneath a hundred feet of water, squeezed by thirty pounds of air pressure to the square inch. But like Tony, Rosen had "wised up." He had never done another honest day's work.

Tony gave no special loyalty to his friends. But Rosen would do absolutely anything for a buck and he had a most unique skill which Tony needed for his plan.

"It's midwinter, for God's sake," Marian grumbled. "Do we need air-conditioning?"

"This is Florida," said Tony.

"I don't care. I'm still cold."

"Shut up," said Tony.

Silence returned, settled over them, broken only by the muted whirl of the conditioner fan.

Up front, Earl Lubeck lighted a cigar and the acrid smoke drifted lazily toward the back seat, causing Marian to wrinkle her nose in distaste. As if in rebuttal, Lubeck sent a great plume of smoke over his shoulder as he turned to peer out the back window. He knew they were not being followed, it was a habit, an automatic gesture to caution.

Lubeck had worked for Tony a long time, as a runner, a bodyguard, strong-arm collector and lieutenant, next in command. But before Tony took him in he had been a longshoreman, a small-town cop and an armored-truck guard.

On a dim, fog-drenched day in San Francisco while

50

his buddies were inside the bank, leaving him to guard the armored truck, he picked up two bulging sacks of cash and calmly carried them around the corner to a waiting car. He had not been seen since.

Lubeck was a thinker, his mind quick and clever. He had a shrewd, larcenous gift of analysis. Give him something as round as a basketball, let him study it long enough and he'd show you that it had an angle.

He was cool, deadly and dependable in a tight situation. But sometimes he relaxed over too many drinks, and then he was not so dependable. The quiet, pensive manner left him. First he became voluble, then argumentative. At such times he had no judgment. He was always right. If you didn't agree with him readily, he became violent. And a violent Earl Lubeck was something to avoid. Everyone became his enemy and nothing would stop him but unconsciousness or death.

Tony was aware of this weakness and would have tossed Earl overboard long ago, but he was too valuable. So there was nothing to do but watch him narrowly, keep him sober—especially when there was a job to be done.

For miles the car glided west, came upon the Hialeah Park race track, slid north again until a small, dark shopping center appeared.

Tony puffed his cigarette into a bright glow and consulted his watch. "Twenty-one minutes before three," he said. "Right on time. Turn left and go down to that gas station, Harry. We'll call from the booth and then come back."

The gas station had long been closed. The booth stood on the apron at the edge of the walk.

Tony felt in his pockets as the Cadillac braked before the booth and Rosen cut the lights. Tony grunted in disgust.

"I got no change," he said. "Wouldn't that be a

hot one? We come all the way out here and nobody's got a dime for the call."

"Here," said Lubeck, reaching back to place a coin in Tony's palm.

Tony shook his head. "A little thing like that. It makes you wonder. Maybe your neck depends on a lousy dime and if you don't have it—"

"I had it, didn't I?" said Lubeck. "It was on my mind and on the way outta the dive I got change."

"Yeah, yeah, you're okay, Earl. Plenty sharp. But I don't like to depend on anyone, even for a dime." He produced a small pocket notebook and held it ready in his hand. "You're sure now, Harry? Everything is set?"

"I'm sure," said Rosen. "You know me, Tony."

"Yeah, well . . ."

Tony ducked out of the car and entered the booth. For a moment he loomed hugely in the light above the phone, his bulk overwhelming the skimpy space. He dialed quickly and opened the door—just enough so that the light winked off.

Rosen had lowered the windows and the rumble of Tony's voice, wordless in the distance, drifted from the booth.

He was back in only a minute. "Move out, Harry. Let's get off the streets. We can't risk being seen now."

"What about after?" Rosen asked as he maneuvered the car around a corner.

"Then it won't matter," Tony replied. "The cops'll have other things on their minds and we'll just slip away in the opposite direction. The idea is to keep moving. If you sit around in a parked car this time of night, you're just law-bait."

"How did you make out on the phone?" Lubeck inquired over his shoulder.

"Hard to say. Oh, I got 'im, all right. But he was

sleepy and I had to keep shoving it home to him. Then he thought I was some crank. I was expecting that. You got to convince 'em with a big play like this. Otherwise you got no leverage, none at all. You're just a voice on the phone. But wait'll tomorrow! Then we'll see, huh?"

Three blocks west of the shopping center on a side street, there was a massive, ugly church. Rosen drifted past it. Then there was the church parking lot and, beside this, an ancient wood-frame, three-story house. The house was ash-colored and peeling. A sign sprouting from the tired tangle of lawn offered the house for rent or sale, furnished.

Rosen pulled into the drive of the old house, circled to the rear and, after a little jockeying in the small space, managed to back the car into a sagging garage.

When Rosen had erased the lights, Tony said, "Let's go! Bring the glasses, Earl. And gimme that flash from the glove compartment, Harry."

"I don't want to go in," said Marian. "I'd just as soon wait in the car."

"No," growled Tony. "Out! And snap it up!"

They climbed a stoop and Tony opened the back door with a key from a ring in his pocket. Entering through the kitchen behind Tony's flash, they skirted the antique furnishings and mounted the stairs.

"Would you believe it?" said Tony conversationally as they reached the first landing and continued upward. "This used to be a cat house. When they closed it I took over, put in a battery of phones and ran a sweet book for a time. Eh, Lubeck? Perfect location. You could spit on the track from here. In those days the town was wide-open. You could buy off the mayor himself. Then *bango*! Down comes the lid. Finished. I mean, you couldn't operate in the open like before.

53

"This old wreck had a bad rep and I couldn't unload it, so I kept it. Now the people who remember what went on here are gone. But the place began to fall apart and now it's a regular firetrap so I still can't move it. I got the lights turned off, but who needs lights for a deal like this?"

Tony led the way to a front bedroom on the third floor. There were two small windows set close together and to these windows Rosen and Lubeck brought chairs. Tony heaved the windows open and seated himself comfortably beside Marian.

"Let's have those glasses, Earl."

"Sure, Tony."

Lubeck removed binoculars from a leather case and passed them. Tony adjusted the glasses to his eyes and began a slow scanning of the area three blocks to the east. The house towered above the lower structures in the lower foreground and the view was unobstructed.

"Good glasses," Tony muttered. "Powerful."

"They should be," said Marian wryly. "Warren paid two hundred for them."

"There," said Tony. "Now I'm getting on target."

In the glasses he had picked up the edge of the shopping center, revealed in soft clarity by the splay of street lamps. Scanning left, he focused upon a bakery, a dry-cleaning shop, a shoe store and a short-order restaurant. All were dark, their polished windows refracting light.

Next a parking lot. Then there was a giant food store, one of a large, statewide, supermarket chain known as the Food Thrift markets. It was the usual long, low building with the all-glass front, the electric glass doors, the paper banners exclaiming boldly over the buys of the day. The market was separate from the other stores, ringed by its own parking area.

Tony got the Food Thrift roof sign in the glasses, dropped below to the big glass doors and held, adjusting to the finest point of focus.

"Target," he said softly.

After a moment he brought the glasses down and turned the flash on the slim solid-gold watch, eyeing the slow progress of the sweep hand.

"Eight minutes to three," he said. "Exactly eight minutes to go."

# – SEVEN –

"EIGHT MINUTES," repeated Lubeck, turning from the window, his long face in shadow. "That's if the timing is right."

"Don't worry," said Rosen. "Just don't worry about the timing."

"So, if it's a couple of minutes, give or take, what's the difference?" Tony said.

"I checked carefully," Rosen answered. "The timing is perfect. And all our watches are in sync."

"Anyway, I don't like it," said Lubeck. "The risk is too big. A thing like this, you can have the whole town breathing down your neck. Give me the old book, anytime—horses, dogs, bolita, any take at all from betting. You get caught and they slap your wrist with a fine or maybe they even toss you in the can for a couple of months or so. Nothing serious. Everyone winks at gambling. You're just a bad boy because the city or the state or the federal isn't getting a bite outta you. But man, they catch you in a squeeze-play like this and they'll cool you for a good twenty or more."

"I agree," said Tony reasonably. "And if I could still run a book with a nice profit, I wouldn't be sitting here now. I'd be asleep, dreaming about tomorrow's collections. But when the new administration came in and they sent that metro clean-up squad after us, the curtain came down and the show was over, buddy.

"They got the money and the men and the power. And you can't buy anyone worth buying any more. You open up, they close you down. You move to a new stall, they smell you out—and fast, so fast you can't keep the customers happy. They can't find you when they want you.

"Then you got the Syndicate. Sometimes you can join 'em, but you can't fight 'em. If you join 'em, you might as well be some goddamn flunkie on a corporation payroll because they'll always eat the cake and feed you the crumbs.

"So what's the answer? You map out a really big scheme like this one. You hit hard and fast and you move on. In maybe three months you got a million bucks in the kick. Then you fold your tents and you steal away. The end. You retire. You live happily ever after, and in damn good style! Sure it's dangerous. Sure the risk is big. But so is the take, brother. We clipped Proctor Drugs for a quarter million, didn't we?"

"Yeah," said Lubeck, looking not quite convinced. "We were lucky. Maybe we should quit after this one."

"No," replied Tony. "But maybe we could raise the ante and then just one more caper would do it— bring us to the mark—that cool million. We'll see how it goes."

Lubeck nodded, chewing his cigar, inspecting the tip and then puffing furiously.

"Does he have to smoke that thing?" said Marian irritably.

"Ask him," Tony cracked.

"I really don't know what I'm doing here," said Marian, her voice edgy, fear-shaded. "You don't need me and I hate being a part of it. Can't I leave, Tony? At least let me wait in the car. It's no thrill for me to watch, you know."

"You'll stay," Tony snapped. "You wanted in. You wanted the pretty toys this kind of dough is gonna buy. So you'll stay. You'll share the risks, you'll pay the tax, baby. No one gets a free ride in this game. Later on I'm gonna need you. I'm gonna put you to work. Meanwhile, you'll stay and get acquainted with the facts of life. Understand?"

"No. But it doesn't matter. I don't have a choice, do I?"

Tony didn't answer. Again he adjusted the glasses.

But Marian did understand one thing. Tony was telling her in his way that she knew too much now. She knew too much to be allowed to sit on the sidelines. He was going to force her to become involved in the development, the action of the plan, because once involved she would not be a threat. Later she could not tell all and plead her personal innocence. She was to be made as guilty as the others.

Why was she here in this room in this musty house with these tense, evil men waiting for the thing to happen? Because of Tony, yes. And her own greed, yes. And maybe, too, because she was as evil as they were. Sure, she had a little more polish, more surface veneer than they did. But underneath, wasn't she just as bad? What about the things she had done which she had never told anyone? Not even Tony.

Tony had remarked, in the most disdainful tone of voice, that this had once been a "cat house," and she had winced. Suppose he found out? Suppose he learned that she had once been a kind of free-lance call girl?

Oh, that was a bad time, a horrible period in her life! Yet, there was an element of excitement in it, of perverse pleasure, too.

It started, like most of her troubles, because of her betting the horses, that consuming habit which she herself could hardly understand. Someone said she was suffering from a guilt complex, that she was trying to punish herself, that she *wanted* to lose. Nonsense like that. Well, of course she didn't want to lose! She wanted to win, win win! She wanted the whole shiny world to tumble into her lap without lifting a hand.

Anita Wymer had told her that she hadn't grown up, that she was still living with a childish dream in which the castle and the gold and the knight on the white steed were all hers for the dreaming. Faced with a reality she couldn't bear, she bet on the horses to perpetuate the dream.

Well, that was closer. Yes, that was more like it.

Anyway, in the end she always lost. And at these times she was desperate, searching madly for a way out. She found it one night in the lobby of a beach hotel, one of those fabulous monuments to the god of sin and sun, fourteen stories of luxury under glass.

She had a date with another of those well-heeled clients she so often met at the office. The man was Chuck Hatley from Chicago, a real estate investor. He bought much property in Miami, flew south at least once a month, employing Burkholtz Title to handle the details of title search and closing.

This night he was due on the 8:20 plane and was to meet her in the lobby of his hotel near nine. Dinner, drinks, a show—the whole bit. It would end in his room, of course But she didn't care, in fact she was counting on it. Chuck was a most superior lover. And Marian was a person who could occasionally become downright nervous if she didn't have her sex in the bank, so to speak.

At ten after nine they were paging her. And at nine-fifteen she was on her own. Chuck had been held up for a couple of days.

Marian was furious. The night was half dead and she was without a date. Furthermore, she was hungry, and she needed a drink—no, a dozen—to make her forget that she owed an impossible tab to the bookie. On top of all that she was in a ravenously sexy mood

—and now there was nothing in the bank for the evening.

She marched into the bar and flopped herself down, ordering a drink. Then another. Some guy a couple of seats away kept leering at her. Well, why not? What the hell.

But when he moved next to her and she found he was a blunt egomaniac who thought her body was his due for the price of two drinks and his winning charm, she became sullen, rebellious. Why should she just give it away to this character?

So when he said, as if it were the unique brainstorm of a genius, "Listen, I've got a bottle of Scotch in my room that's older than my grandmother. Why don't we tie one on, just the two of us?" she answered: "Why, I'd just love to! But I can't. I was supposed to meet a guy here who owes me some money. I'm just a working girl, you know, a secretary. I did a whole batch of typing for this guy and now I need the money. I'm not going anywhere until I get it."

"Oh . . . oh, I see. Well, how much did this fella owe you?"

"Ninety-eight dollars and change. You might as well call it a hundred," she said.

"And if you had this mony you could leave with me?"

"I guess so. Sure, why not? It wasn't a date or anything."

He gave her the hundred and she went up to his room and he pretended he believed her and it all went off very smoothly.

So three or four times a week she went to different plush hotels and worked the same gimmick, screening her men so she didn't get some repulsive slob. Sometimes it was exciting and sometimes it was degrading. But oh, how profitable! And quite foolproof. Never did she proposition anyone—so how could she get caught?

She was practically ready to give up her job, the money was so easy. But then she had a slow night and she took a chance on a guy who told her he had the cash in his room. He didn't. Or, if he did, he wasn't about to produce it. He was a phony! She wanted out.

He grabbed her and she resisted. That was when he ripped her clothes and beat her so badly she couldn't show herself at work for a week, had to play sick. And that was also the end of her short career as a call girl. She soon met Tony and decided he was a safer way out.

Safer? Maybe he wouldn't beat her, but Tony's way of living was anything but safe.

"One minute," said Tony. "One minute to three." Again he raised the glasses and brought the Food Thrift market into focus.

"Oh Christ!" Lubeck grumbled. "I don't like it. I've got a feeling about this one."

"There's a church next door," said Tony. "Go and pray. Meanwhile, shut up."

"You want me to give you the countdown, Tony?" asked Rosen.

"Yeah yeah. What is it now?"

"Twenty-two seconds," Rosen announced.

"What will happen?" Marian asked in a tremulous voice.

No one answered. Tension was nearly palpable in the room.

"Five seconds," Rosen called. "Four-three-two-one."

In the binoculars Tony saw nothing but the shadowy framework of the building, the dim luster of glass.

"Well," he said, "where's the action, Rosen? I thought you had this thing figured for—"

Suddenly a thunderous blast shattered the morning. In the glasses Tony saw the supermarket disintegrate, vomiting flame and smoke, the explosion hurling fragments into the air, showering them down upon the parking area.

Now there was no need of magnification. They could all see with naked eyes. The flames which followed the blast lighted the sky with their awesome red-white beauty.

"I told you, I told you!" cried Rosen proudly. "I wasn't a powder monkey for nothing, eh, Tony? Right on time! Maybe ten seconds late, that's all!"

"You'll get a medal," Tony growled. "Now c'mon. C'mon, let's move outta here!"

# – EIGHT –

THIRTY MINUTES LATER, the blue Cadillac entered downtown Miami. It breezed along Biscayne Boulevard, anonymous in the late cluster of vehicles.

On the back seat, his arm draped casually over Marian's shoulder, Tony yawned.

He said, "Harry, stop in front of that hamburger joint on the corner. Pick up a sack of burgers, some fries and coffee all around."

"I'm not hungry," said Marian.

"Meanwhile," Tony continued, "I'll make another call to Stienmetz. By this time he's got the message, eh? He knows we play for keeps."

"Maybe he's out," Lubeck offered. "Maybe he went down to see what's left of his food barn."

"Yeah, maybe," answered Tony, as Rosen drew up at the curb. "But I doubt it. All that confusion, they probably took a while phoning him the score."

Accepting another dime from Lubeck, Tony hoisted his bulk from the car and strode toward the outdoor booth nudging the hamburger stand. He flipped the pages of his pocket notebook, fed the coin and dialed. The line was busy. He kept trying until he heard the ring.

"Yes?"

"Stienmetz?"

"Yes, yes. What now?" The voice of David Stienmetz, president and founder of Food Thrift markets, crackled across the line.

"I hear you got a fire sale goin' for you at the Hialeah store, Stienmetz. What're you sellin'—charcoal?"

"I'm selling rope to hang you with, you filthy

bastard! I recognize your voice. Who are you, any-way?"

"You can call me Greengold, pal, because this is Operation Green-Gold, get it? And I wanna be countin' a whole pile of that green tonight, or we'll blast another store into Shredded Wheat!"

"Not a cent, you psycho creep! When you blew up that market you started the biggest manhunt in the history of Florida. I'll have you and your hoods caged in twenty-four hours!"

"Aw, now you got me trembling all over. I'm so scared I can hardly hold the phone. Listen Stienmetz, cut the comedy and let's talk business. How many stores you got? Twenty-eight in this county alone —right? Another couple dozen in Broward County, so forth all the way to Jacksonville. So which one'll be next? You gonna cover 'em all? Never, Buster, never! You gonna shut down? I don't think so. The customers would hike on over to A & P or Kwick Check, one of the other chains. A lot of 'em would never come back. Meantime, how much would it cost you a day? A hundred grand wouldn't touch it.

"Then you got the scare problem to worry about. People read in the papers we're blowin' up your mar-kets, they get the shakes. Because right while they're shoppin' at Food Thrift the bomb might go off and blast 'em to hell. You think they'll risk it? Wait 'n see. One more blow and you couldn't trap three cus-tomers in one of them stores if you sold steak a penny a pound."

Tony inspected his watch. Though he knew a trace would take longer, he would not gamble on talking over two minutes.

"How much?" said Stienmetz after a heavy silence.

"Three hundred thousand."

"Three hundred thou—not a chance! We won't pay it!"

"You'll pay it all right, and this is how you'll deliver. Listen good, because I'm only gonna say it once. Tonight at seven sharp we'll send a messenger to your house for the dough. Three hundred grand in hundreds—*old* hundreds, not a new bill in the bunch. Pack the money in a brief case and band it in thirty stacks, ten thousand to a stack.

"Now this messenger will be a flunky. He won't know one goddamn thing about the deal, just that he's out to pick up a case and deliver it somewhere. So don't try havin' the cops sweat him and don't hold him or the game is called. Ditto if you have him followed. No cops—not one, or we wreck another store. Get me?"

"Yes, but let me tell *you* something! I'll have you—"

"Now this messenger will say like this: 'My name is Speedy and Mr. Greengold sent me for the samples.' You don't deliver unless you get that line—'My name is Speedy and Mr. Greengold sent me for the samples.'

"Seven sharp, Stienmetz. Have the cash ready, or we'll make splinters outta the whole chain all the way to Jacksonville."

"Now you wait a minute, you dirty punk! Are you crazy? We can't get hold of that kind of money on such short notice. My God, we—"

"You better deliver, chum. Right on time!"

Tony slapped the receiver down. For a moment he stood in a thoughtful attitude, head cocked as if he might be listening to a distant sound. Then he left the booth.

The car eased gently from the curb, again becoming lost in southbound traffic. Tony leaned back comfortably, munching a hamburger, sipping coffee, occasionally crowding his mouth with a handful of

French fries scooped from the greasy white bag in his lap.

No one spoke. Tony did not like to talk when he was eating, though this had nothing to do with good manners. He simply would not permit anyone to distract him from his pleasurable absorption with food.

The Cadillac paused as Rosen paid the toll at the entrance gate to Biscayne Key, then skimmed on again.

Tony smiled, a narrow secret smile, remembering his promise to exact his own tolls from all the fat monarchs of the world in which he found himself. He felt expansive, vastly confident and superior. He had an enormous sense of well-being.

After a while he finished eating and tossed the empty paper bag and coffee container out the window. The wind hurled these behind, sucking them into the night, at last depositing them at the base of a sign which read: DUMPING REFUSE ALONG HIGHWAY FORBIDDEN UNDER PENALTY OF FINES UP TO $100.

Tony's well-being included a warm current of sexual desire. His groin felt lazily tumescent. In the dark his hand came up beneath Marian's breast and closed around it.

"Don't," she whispered. "Not now, Tony. I'm not in the mood."

Tony ignored her. His other hand snaked beneath her skirt and began a sinuous path upward over her thigh. For a moment she clamped her legs together and tried to move them sideways out of his grasp. But Tony found resistance fascinating and, wedging his hand between her legs, forced it onward.

Suddenly she relaxed, her head fell to his shoulder with a little sigh of pleasure. "But won't they see us," she whispered in his ear.

Tony shrugged. "Who cares?" He chuckled.

"Make 'em sweat a little, huh? It might be kinda fun."
So saying, he took her hand and pressed it solidly
against his crotch. . . .

Lubeck was the first to voice alarm as they slid
around a corner and the house became visible a block
away, a bold island of light set against the darkness
of the dwellings surrounding it.

"Hey!" he bawled. "F'crissake, look at that! Who
turned the goddamn lights on in the house?"

Tony quickly undid himself from Marian's embrace. Sitting up, he gaped in astonishment.

"Maybe the cops," he muttered. "I don't know
how, but maybe the cops. Gun past on the double,
Harry. We'll have a look."

His hand darted to his pocket and came up with
a .38 automatic. He held it poised, hooded eyes probing house and grounds as they flew past.

"Nothing," he said. "Anyway, would the cops set
up a stake-out and leave the goddamn lights torching?
Let's go back. Fast, Harry, fast! I can smell trouble."

Tony got to the closet first and spied the note.
He ripped it away and gulped the contents at a
glance. Getting the drift immediately, he reached
for the closet door and nearly tore it from the hinges.

"Gone!" he thundered. "Gone, gone, gone!" His
big fist smashed against the door panel and splintered
it. He plucked the note from the floor where he had
dropped it and this time read it with more care.

"You!" he shouted, aiming a finger at Marian.
"You! You're the cause of this. A quarter million
bucks out the goddamn window because of a lousy
dame!"

He advanced two steps and walloped her across
the face with his open hand. She fell sideways and
crumpled to the floor, whimpering, blood showing
at a corner of her mouth.

Tony was a muscled giant standing over her, a

67

nerve twitching his eye. "All right, all right," he said in a dark, soft voice, terrible with menace. "So you cost me a quarter million and you're not worth fifty bucks, you cheap slut! But you're gonna help me get that dough back. And then I'm gonna do you just one more favor—I'm gonna make you a widow!"

# – NINE –

Earlier, Warren Emrick had been locked in his hotel room thinking about the money. He lay fully dressed upon the bed, a forgotten cigarette drooping from a corner of his mouth, a new fifth of Canadian Club resting untouched beside him on a night table.

The suitcase yawned from a chair across the room, revealing a welter of currency. Warren stared at the money and pondered the problems it created. Though he was not excessively brave, he wasn't afraid of Tony Viani and his stooges. This was partly because his hate was bigger than fear and partly because he no longer gave a particular damn what happened to him.

He was full of dead and bitter things which corrupted his will and dissipated his spirit. Still, he was basically a man of good judgment. And now that he felt somewhat vindicated, he began to consider his actions in a more careful light.

At first, caught by a reckless, vengeful impulse, it had seemed a superb idea to exchange that quarter million of Tony Viani's for Marian—in payment for treachery and the theft of his forty-seven thousand. The irony of it was marvelous, and such a gift of riches was enormously tempting. But he had not reckoned with the habit patterns of a lifetime.

It would certainly be a kind of stealing to keep more than the forty-seven thousand and one did not become a thief overnight. One could not develop long habits of discriminate behavior and then put them aside with a careless shrug. One could, of course, do many things inconsistent with his character on impulse—driven by emotions which distorted perspective. But these were only temporary aberrations.

So now, in a calmer more thoughtful mood, it seemed to Warren that he had made a mistake. He should have taken only the money which was his. Then he should have cornered this Viani, at a time when the odds were not three to one in Viani's favor, and clobbered him witless!

It was not too late, though he would have to move cautiously. Tony would certainly be carrying a gun, and he would probably use it. And in spite of his former abandon, Warren was not going to kill or be killed in an idiot attempt at vengeance now that he had regained some of his sanity.

Really, why should he destroy what was left of his life in a moment of crazy violence? What he wanted was his money and the satisfaction of mauling Viani so that he would never forget. As a bonus he might uncover the truth behind that quarter million. Surely the bastard wouldn't be in possession of that kind of dough and an arsenal of guns unless he was a very bad boy. So it was quite possible that he could put Viani in a cell for a few years where he would have time to think over the miscalculation he made when he figured he could sucker Warren out of his wife and his lifetime savings.

The police would be delighted with such a prize, especially if Warren could furnish them with enough information for a conviction. God, even the tax boys would take a very dim view of all that unreported cash!

And what of Marian? He could make up his mind that she was a vicious tramp and not worthy of tears or violence. Or he could find a more subtle way to settle with her.

He would have to puzzle that out later. Mean-

70

while there were things to be done. He would have
to get a line on Tony Viani, and he would have to do
it fast. Viani would be in a highly nervous state and
he might jump in any direction. Warren couldn't tell
what he might do next—not without a better understanding of the sort of creep he was. One thing he
could predict—Viani would be hunting for a guy
named Warren Emrick and a quarter of a million
bucks.

Warren reached for a tray and crushed his cigarette decisively. He found Anita Wymer's phone
number and gave it to the operator. He glanced at
his watch. It was just after eleven and it was unlikely
that Wymer would be home.

To his surprise she answered at once. Her voice
sounded edgy. Abruptly he changed his mind and
hung up. She might give him the brush on the phone.
Better to appear in person.

Wymer was important to him now, more so than
ever. She was the only link. She might furnish him
with enough clues to sink Viani and company. She
would probably be a most unwilling pigeon, but now
he had fresh ammunition and there were certain pres-
sures he could bring to bear.

He did not understand the relationship between
Wymer and Marian. He could find no basis for the
apparent bond which held them and caused Anita to
be so fiercely protective. Even less could he fathom
the tie between Wymer and Viani. But then, there
was a time when Marian displayed the same face of
innocence.

Warren climbed out of bed and scanned the room
for a place to hide the currency. He discarded several
possibilities because of their space limitations. Only
the obvious enclosures would hold that much paper.

Well, was he really concerned with the cash in
excess of his own forty-seven thousand? Only in so

71

much as it could be used to convict Viani. With a shrug he counted the portion which was his and crossed with it to the air-conditioner, presently out of use in the cooler climate of winter.

He removed the vented cover and the filter screen. Behind this was the cavity housing the fan. There was enough room, though it was a tight squeeze. After stashing the bills he replaced the screen and cover. He returned to the suitcase and piled clothing on top of the remaining loot and weapons. He stowed the case beneath the bed, knowing it would not be disturbed because only Viani and his tribe were aware that the money existed. Hiding his own share was merely an extra precaution against the freak circumstance of a hotel robbery.

He cut the lights and went out, locking the room behind him. In fifteen minutes he was again standing before Anita Wymer's door.

She answered in a matter of seconds, opening the door to the limits of a chain. She peeped out at him with narrowed eyes, her expression wary. There was a glimpse of pale blue negligée.

"Again!" she said sharply. "What do you want now?"

"I thought you were going to a party."

"There was no party. It was an excuse. And if you don't tell me what you're doing here at this hour I'm going to close this door in your face and call the police."

"I want to talk to you."

"Don't be absurd."

"About Tony Viani."

There was a taught silence. "Well, I knew you would find out sooner or later. What about Tony?"

"He's a very bad boy and he's in trouble."

"With the police?"

"With me."

72

She snorted. "Obviously you haven't met Tony. You're a child in the dark aiming a toy gun at a tiger." She laughed unpleasantly, a chill sound, both mocking and piteous. "You'd better go home, my friend. While you can. Forget about Tony—and Marian. Let the dead bury their dead—know what I mean?"

There was a grim sincerity about her, a frightening undertone of conviction. Suddenly he knew she was right. He should take his money and he should go home and try to forget. But of course he wouldn't. He was driven by pride and the need to maintain the image of himself as a man.

"Never mind," he said. "You seem like a pretty decent sort and I thought you might help me. But I'll just run along and tell my troubles to the police. They have real guns and sometimes they're pretty good with tigers, even in the dark. Besides, I have some new light I can throw on Tony for them."

"What could you possibly tell the police that could hurt Tony?"

"Ahh. Now you're interested!"

Behind the door she shifted her position and peered at him intently. "I'm only curious. Why should I care what happens to Tony?"

"I've been wondering about that." He smiled wryly. "Anyway, when Tony falls, you and Marian might just stumble a bit, don't you think? That is, if you don't go down with him. God knows what small fish might get caught in the net, innocent or not. Am I beginning to make sense?"

"What do you want from me?" she said after a thoughtful space.

"Just conversation—if you'll open the door so I can come in and ask a few polite questions."

"The next time I open this door," she answered bitterly, "it will be morning and I'll be on my way

73

to work and you'd better not be around. I've had experience with your 'polite' questions."

He shrugged. "There are other ways. Just trying to save time. Well, see you around. Maybe down at the police station, huh?"

"Wait. Drive two blocks north along the bay," she commanded. "There's a bar called The Mast. Take a booth. I'll meet you there in fifteen minutes."

She closed the door firmly.

The Mast was a dim rectangular den, carelessly simulating the interior of an ancient schooner. Tight rows of booths lined the water-view side of the building, and in one of these Warren waited, sipping a Black Russian strong enough to loosen the soles of his shoes by osmosis.

He was turning from the soft flicker of lights across the bay, preparing to order a fresh drink, when Anita appeared. She was wearing a gold-mesh sweater and a silky black hobble skirt. The ensemble clung to the ripe hills and graceful valleys of her lush terrain. She came toward him with brisk, clever little steps that caused her tawny hair to sway rhythmically against her shoulders.

It was as if he saw her for the first time. He was a traveler returning over the same route, astonished that in his earlier distraction he could have missed the delicate beauty of her landscape.

She sat down with the barest hint of a smile, her features abstract, shadowed by the tension of some secret turmoil.

"What is that you're drinking?" she asked.

"A Black Russian."

"I've never had one."

"They make them of vodka and a coffee liqueur."

"Are they strong?"

"Herculean."

"I'll try one."

74

"A true gambler." He signaled the waiter to bring two of the same. "You won't be sorry. It's not a drink, it's a sort of creeping paralysis. After the second one you can't even remember what you're trying to forget."

She smiled wanly. "How tall and brave and carefree are the people poured from bottles," she said. "Alcohol, when it's done with you, is like a dirty street in harsh sunlight right after an impossibly romantic movie."

"That's good," he said. "That's very sensitive. I don't come up with deep comparisons that easily."

"Neither do I. I put things like that together after a lot of thought in my quiet hours. Then I hurl them out at little games and parties as if they were quick adlibs from a fertile brain."

"You've just revealed your secret," he said. "Thus your honesty remains intact."

"Flattery will get you no answers. Not one."

"Then you do have answers?"

"No comment."

"If not, why did you come?"

"Well, I . . ."

The waiter brought the drinks and they were silent until he had gone.

"I came because I don't want you to go do anything foolish that might endanger—"

"That might endanger who? Me? The little boy in the dark with the toy gun?"

She sipped her drink, her expression neither approving nor disapproving of it. "Well, if I'm going to forgive your acrobatics with me this evening, I really have nothing against you. So I wouldn't want to see you hurt, naturally. But I don't know you well enough to care as much about what happens to you as certain others."

"Marian? Tony?"

75

"Marian, yes. Tony also. Because what happens to him will affect Marian and—"

"You?"

"I suppose so. Yes, I'm only human. I'm not looking for trouble."

"Then you must be involved."

"I didn't say that! I'm no more involved than a man sitting at a lunch counter is involved in an accident which happens outside on the street as he watches through the window. Still, a car out of control could crash through that window, and kill him."

"Isn't that about what I said awhile ago? The innocent bystander?"

Her thin smile was vague, detached. He had the feeling that her real personality was not there at all, except in the most mechanical sense.

"Aside from stealing wives," he said, "and conning them into absconding with hubbies' bank acount, what kind of racket is lover-boy Viani operating?"

"Who told you he had a racket?"

"Oh, c'mon, Anita, let's not play games!"

"Well, he's a bookie, a kind of super bookie. Is that so terrible?"

"Does the modern bookie have a whole arsenal of guns?"

She stared at him blankly.

"Maybe Tony has a sideline—like bank robbing."

"I don't know much about Tony," she answered gravely. "He certainly ran a book. I know several people who placed bets with him—or his runners. Then he left town and I lost track of him. Not so long ago he returned. He gave me a call and I met him for lunch. But he was really interested in Marian and we had very little else in common. Exactly what he does now, I wouldn't know. He doesn't talk about his business, and anyone who has nerve enough to ask questions is either stupid or a lot braver than I am."

76

"But you like him. You think he's a great guy."

She took a long drag on her cigarette, removed a shard of tobacco from the dainty tip of her tongue. "I wouldn't say that I like him. I respect him—the way you would respect a loaded shotgun. I also find him fascinating—in the same way. What's more, I owe him a great deal."

"And Marian? She's the worst kind of tramp. What is it that makes you so uncompromisingly loyal to her? What is *her* fascination?"

"You answer that," she said with a biting smile. "You married her, didn't you?"

"Sure. But at the time I thought she was a woman, not a snake. She kept her fangs well hidden to the last."

"Marian and I worked in the same office. We dated together. We became good friends."

"That's no answer," he snorted.

"My God, you're persistent."

"You bet. And you ain't seen nothin' yet. I'm going to have my day in court and I'm not leaving until I do, one way or another."

She smashed her cigarette. "All right, all right! So I don't really like Marian at all. She's a slick phony, she's cheap and she's an incurable liar. I never believed her story about inheriting money or the sad tale about having to escape from you because you were such a dreadful monster. I knew she had the hots for Tony and she would run any time he whistled. There's a certain type of female who looks and acts like a prissy, tea-sipping member of the royal family while underneath she's an alley cat wailing for a crude Tom just like herself. That's Marian. And I knew it long before you did. You should have met me years ago. I'd have put you on the right train."

"That's better! Now I'm beginning to like you."

"But," she continued, "Marian once did me a very big favor. And favor is a mild word. I owe her a certain loyalty, though you can stretch loyalty so tight that it snaps right back in your face."

She swallowed, as if downing some bitter medicine, and stared off at the dark blanket of water.

"You seem to be in debt everywhere," Warren mused. "Tony Viani, now Marian."

She turned back. For a moment she fixed him with a searching gaze. "It's all part of the same evil complex created by Tony. He feeds you with one hand and chains you with the other—the one he hides behind his back." She sighed. "I guess it won't do any harm to tell you about it."

"It can do a lot of good! We might be able to help each other."

*At last*, he thought. *She's going to stop covering up and tell the truth!*

# – TEN –

"YOU HAVE TO UNDERSTAND ABOUT MY BROTHER, Randy," Anita began. "He has everything to do with my present attitude toward Marian and Tony.

"It goes back to the time my brother was drafted into the army. He's twenty-four now, very old and worldly wise for his age. But he seemed just a kid when he put on his uniform a few years ago. In those days he was sensitive. And he was weak—always looking for a soft berth and a free ride. Anyway, he despised the army and after a series of escapades which ended in the guard house, he deserted. Eventually they caught him and he went to prison for a short period. There, he became tough and cynical and he got friendly with some cons who didn't exactly improve him any.

"When he was released he wouldn't go to college and he wouldn't work. He didn't do anything but 'ball it up,' as he would say—tall drinks and tall women with round heels. He always seemed to have money which he claimed he won at poker, crap, the horses and so on. He was a sullen, arrogant brat and I detested and loved him at the same time. He lived with me because my parents are hard-heads who wouldn't tolerate him after a few feeble tries at rebuilding him in their image. I tried to help Randy without talking down to him, and every now and then he showed signs of improvement.

"Then one night there was a hold-up at one of those super liquor stores, a big cut-rate place that's so busy there are three clerks on every shift, all girls. The owner is usually around, but on this Saturday

79

night he had taken a couple of hours off to go to his own birthday party, so the girls were alone when these two characters walked in waving guns.

"They were young guys, not much older than my brother. First they made the girls lock up the store and darken it. By then it was near closing time anyway, and no one was apt to be very suspicious. Well, they scooped up the money, a big haul because it was Saturday and the registers had been clanging madly all day and evening. And then they forced those girls into the back room, the storeroom, where they ripped their clothes off and raped them. In fact those animals made the girls do some things which the papers called too obscene to print. One of the girls put up a fight and she was beaten unconscious.

"Finally they locked the girls in that storeroom, grabbed all the booze they could carry and escaped. But they were ex-cons and the girls identified them from pictures in a mug book. Three nights later they were caught celebrating in a dive where they usually hung out with an assortment of free-wheeling dames.

"When they were caught, Randy, my brother, was with them."

She paused, puffed her cigarette, drank. She watched his face for a reaction.

"I saw it coming," said Warren. "Go on."

"Well, these sterling playmates of my brother swore he was with them on the night of the hold-up and rape. They said Randy was the lookout man, the driver, and it was his car that was used in the getaway. One of the ex-cons had served time with my brother—and that was bad, though Randy denied everything.

"Furthermore, some of the booze from the store was found in the trunk of his car, and he had over eight hundred dollars cash in his wallet. He explained that he won the liquor and the money from these hoods in a card game. But of course the cops laughed him right into a cell. He was indicted with the others and held for trial.

"At this point my family couldn't even remember his first name and would never admit his last. So it was all up to me. I didn't know where to turn. I didn't even have the money to make bail.

"Then I thought of Marian. She was all but married to Tony and I knew he had all kinds of connections and might be able to steer me to one of those sharpies who lend money at cutthroat interest. Forty, fifty per cent, whatever it was, I didn't care. I needed a good lawyer and then there was the bail. So I told Marian the whole story and asked her if she could get Tony to introduce me to a loan shark. I had tried the banks and the finance companies and they had brushed me with the sort of polite smiles that are more like sneers.

"I didn't really expect much help from Marian because she seldom put herself out unless there was something in it for her. But, to my surprise, she said not to worry about anything, she would persuade Tony to look into my brother's case and see if he couldn't get Randy off the hook.

"Well, in a few words, Tony called me and said he was sending his own lawyer down to see Randy and that my brother would be out in a few hours. He was, too! He was there when I got home that night. Next thing you know, those cons had changed their story. They admitted Randy wasn't along with them on the night of the robbery after all. And why did they frame him? A grudge. They were furious because he won most of the money they had stolen from the liquor store.

"So the D.A. got the indictment nullified and the charges were dropped for lack of evidence. Of course Tony was behind it. He got word to those thugs that if they didn't reverse their story they'd never leave prison alive. His pals on the inside would see to it. And now maybe you understand why I owe so much to Marian and Tony."

Warren nodded. "I get the picture. And what of your brother? Do you think he was guilty?"

She chewed her lip. "I know he was guilty. He came home loaded one night and confessed the whole thing to me. He bragged about it. We had a big scene and the next day he moved out."

"What's he doing now?"

"Tony gave him a job as a glorified errand boy for a time. Then Tony left and Randy amazed me by getting married to a nice, wholesome little girl whose father owns a taxi cab company. The girl was a good influence it seems, because Randy settled down and now he's a dispatcher for his father-in-law's cab company. Stays out of trouble so far as I know. But he never forgot Tony, still thinks he's a god and can do no wrong."

They were silent for awhile. Then Warren asked, "Do you really think Tony Viani is still just a big-time bookie?"

She shook her head. "No, not any more. I asked Marian and she said he's out of the gambling racket. In this town the risk is too great these days."

"In that case, what kind of swindle would bring him a quarter of a million bucks cash?"

"A quarter of a million! I can't imagine. What makes you think he has that kind of money?"

"I saw it with my own eyes."

He went on to relate the events of the evening. It could do no harm since she could tell Tony nothing which he would not soon know himself first-hand. As a matter of precaution, he did not tell her where he had hidden the money.

When he had finished she said, "God, Almighty, if you don't catch the next plane going anywhere, you're the biggest damn fool who ever lived! You're in more danger than I could hope to make you understand. Run out of here. Don't tell me where you're going—just go!"

He smiled. "You know I won't do that. Besides, Viani is not superhuman. He's just a man. I'm going to outguess and outthink him all the way. And if not, what's the worst that can happen to me?"

"You can die very suddenly."

"Exactly. And is that so bad?"

"Did you really care that much about her?"

He shrugged. "Let's say that I'm completely disenchanted with just about everything I used to hold so goddamn sacred."

"You'll get over it in time. And then you'll want to live as much as ever."

"Maybe. Right now I only want to drink the bittersweet nectar of revenge. Just give me a foot in the door so I can nail Viani to my cross. What's he up to? You must have some idea. Marian has a careless tongue. She never could keep a secret."

"True. But when her life's at stake, even she can keep a secret. Tony would strangle his own mother if she crossed him. Marian did say that Tony had a fantastic scheme for making money in bales and that when this scheme made them rich in the next few weeks, Tony was going to retire and they were going to live in respectable splendor the rest of their lives."

"Nothing else?"

"Nothing."

"Then, why were you so worried that everyone, including yourself, would get into trouble if I went to the police?"

"Well, naturally I knew Tony wasn't running a

bingo game to make himself rich. If he got arrested, I might get hurt by association. I've been out with Tony and his bunch from time to time."

"Have you? That surprises me."

"It does? That's because you're not a secretary making seventy-five a week, Miami scale. That's what Food Thrift pays me for being Girl Friday to their general manager. And when I go out with the Viani troop, which includes Tony, his two pals and Marian, Tony has a habit of slipping a fifty or a hundred dollar bill into my purse. And don't raise your eyebrows, there are no sneaky obligations. I make gay faces and gay sounds, I laugh at their crude corn—but I go home alone.

"Why Tony helps me is a mystery. He pretends it's just because he likes me. I seem to be getting a free ride. Actually, I have the feeling that I'm being buttered up and that one day Tony will swallow me whole."

Warren nodded. "You can count on it. But just because you've been around with that Viani bunch isn't enough to get you into any serious trouble, no matter what game they're playing. You're holding out. There must be something more."

She studied her glass, twirling it thoughtfully. She drank. "Say, did I tell you? These Black Russians are good! And I'll bet the Russians never heard of them."

"No, the Russians couldn't afford them. And you're stalling."

She frowned, then looked up suddenly. "All right, I'm going to trust you. Mostly because I don't have another soul to talk to about this and it's a lonely burden to carry."

"I understand all about lonely burdens. Shoot."

"Well, my real problem is Randy. I think he's involved and I'm only going along with Tony so I can find out how and why. You see, I was invited to a party at Tony's one night last week. I arrived a bit early, just in time to see Randy leaving.

"I asked him what he was doing there and he said, just a drink with an old friend. Tony was like a father to him. Didn't Tony come through when he could have gone to prison for God knows how many years? Didn't Tony save him? Sure, and that's the sort of hero worship that will trap Randy into another bad jam. Randy was doing fine until Tony came back. Now I'm worried."

Warren said, "Maybe there's nothing to it. Maybe he *was* just having a friendly drink with Viani."

"Never. Tony does not waste time with friendly drinks. There's a sly motive behind every move he makes. If he invited Randy to his house it was to use him as a part of some evil scheme."

She gulped her drink. When she put the glass down, her eyes were misty and withdrawn. "Tony Viani is a disease. He infects everyone he touches. Like all diseases, he's got to be isolated, or destroyed. Now, come on, I think it's time you took me home."

# – ELEVEN –

Tony Viani glared down at the others seated around the kitchen table. He stood leaning toward them across the back of a chair, his heavy features reflecting the dark, brooding threat of his anger. He pushed his coffee cup aside and, like the gavel of an irate judge, the hairy knob of his big fist pounded the table for attention.

"Now goddamn it," he said. "there's got to be an answer! And we're gonna come up with that answer if we have to kick this around till dawn!"

"Yeah, and that's not far away," said Harry Rosen. He gulped coffee, glancing at his watch. "It's a quarter to four already."

"That's the point," Tony said. "We're gonna have to jump Emrick in a hurry, before he gets outta town."

"First we gotta find him," said Earl Lubeck. "It's one helluva big city, you know."

Tony's eyes narrowed as they fell upon Marian. She had changed into a sweater and skirt and now she sat staring down meekly into her coffee, as if even to look at Tony might remind him of his conviction that she was the cause of his trouble.

"Don't just sit there, you stupid bitch!" Viani growled. "You know this guy, you played footsy with him for three years—so think like he thinks. Where would he go with that quarter million?"

"I don't know," said Marian, glancing up cautiously. "He might have been satisfied. He might have gone back to New York. If not, he'll hang around to see what else he can do to you—and me. If I know him, he probably wants to—"

"Wants to what!"

"Wants to beat you up."

"Me! Emrick beat *me* up?" Tony's laughter, ponderous as the roll of a kettle drum, filled the room. "Jesus Christ, I'd like to see him try. You find the bastard and make an appointment, huh, baby? I'll open him up like an autopsy with my bare hands."

"I wouldn't underestimate him," said Marian. "He's no flabby weakling. He was once Golden Gloves champion."

"Golden Gloves!" Tony snorted. "I suppose he works out at the Athletic Club with the rest of those white-collar pansies. You've got a lot to learn, kiddo. When your boy falls dead he won't be wearin' gloves. And because *you* underestimated him and it cost me a fortune, I'm gonna teach you a few things, too. Wait 'n see!"

"I was only trying to help," said Marian weakly.

"I think we should blow to some other part of town," Lubeck suggested. "This Emrick knows where we are and he might tip the cops."

"Why should he tip the cops?" Tony reasoned. "In the first place he's got all that loot he stole from us and he couldn't keep it if he brought the law. Second, he don't have an idea what we're doin'. So what's he gonna talk about?

"Now this crappy chit-chat is getting nowhere. Let's start from the beginning. How did Emrick find us? If we know that we should be able to find him." Viani massaged his nose with a thick finger and washed his mouth with coffee. "All right, so this wise guy is kind of clever, we'll say. He's a real bright boy and we give him a gold star for brains, but he's no psychic genius. He don't look into a crystal ball and see us here in this house like on TV.

Hell no! What's more, he didn't have clue one that I know of." He threw a brief, probing look at Marian. "So someone had to tell him where to find us."

"Right," said Lubeck. "Now all you got to do is call off the names of everyone who knew about this pad and eliminate."

"Okay!" Tony banged his cup down. "That's it! Now there's the three of you here to start with. Did one of you open your trap anywhere? Harry?"

"Not me, Tony."

"Earl?

"You think I'm crazy?"

"Yeah, when you're drunk."

"The answer is no, Tony. Drunk or sober, n-o."

"Marian?"

"Of course not. You know me, Tony."

"Damn right. And that's why I'm askin'. So think hard."

"Well, naturally I didn't even hint to Warren. You know that."

"Don't tell me what I know! Did you open your trap to anyone else?"

"You have my word, Tony."

"Your word," he sneered. "Okay, so who does that leave? The kid, Randy? Not a chance. You could cut his ears off and he wouldn't squeal. Besides, how would he ever come in contact with Emrick?"

"What about the sister?" asked Earl Lubeck.

"Anita? She's practically on the payroll," Tony replied.

"She may be on the payroll," Rosen contributed, "but she don't know there's anything she's got to hide—nothin' more than to keep Emrick off Marian's neck. You want my opinion, I think she's a snooty bitch who only puts out for Yale and Harvard grads.

You got to show 'er the key—you know, the ole Phi Beta Kappa.

"Spit out the sour grapes and shut up," Tony snapped. "You had a lotta laughs with Wymer. You got no kick."

"Yeah, I was laughin' all the way to her door. Then I was cryin'. Besides, she's bein' paid to laugh. What a joke that is. A dollar a chuckle."

"I pay 'er because I want her to hop at the right time," Tony came back. "I'm gonna need her, like tomorrow morning when Marian calls her at Food Thrift and pumps her about the next move Stienmetz is gonna make. Hell, we got a spy in the enemy camp."

"Still, I think Harry is right," Lubeck said. "She's an outsider and she's dangerous to the whole operation. We've checked everyone who knew this address and she's the only logical possibility."

"Marian," asked Tony, "did Emrick know your friend Anita?"

"No. I don't think I ever mentioned her. I did get a couple of letters from her. But he's not the type who would read my mail."

"Yeah? Well, I wouldn't lay odds. Anyway, he knew you were from Miami and he knew you had friends here. He'd try to get a lead through them. You must have told him a few things—where you worked, stuff like that."

"Yes, I told him where I worked, though I doubt if he remembered."

"It doesn't matter," said Tony. "He came down here and somehow he got to Anita. If not, who else? She has to be the one."

"She'd never talk," said Marian. "Never. I made her promise."

"Oh? So you did think maybe he'd get in touch with her, didn't you?"

89

"Well," said Marian warily, "there was always an off-chance he might locate her, so I asked her to play dumb. I was just being careful, Tony, and smart."

"You're smart all right. You left a trail as big as the Grand Canyon. If I wasn't afraid you'd leak all over the place, I'd toss you out on your can right now."

He turned to Lubeck. "You and Harry hold the fort here. I'm gonna go over and have a little chat with Anita."

"At this hour?" said Lubeck.

"At this hour, buddy."

"You want us to come along?" asked Rosen.

"No. I've got an angle. I'll do better alone. You guys just take care of Marian. See that she don't go anywhere. Even if you have to sleep with her, see that she don't leave the house."

"Tony!" cried Marian, gaping in shock, her rich mouth an open wound.

"You mean that?" said Lubeck, grinning lewdly and winking at Rosen. "You mean that, Tony?"

"Take it any way you like," said Viani coolly. He gave Marian a hard, calculating look in which there was the barest trace of a smile. Then he strode from the room.

There was the sound of the door closing and then the polite murmur of the Cadillac departing.

Earl and Harry Rosen again exchanged glances. They wore the sneaky faces of schoolboys about to commit some naughty prank, though undecided as to how they should begin.

Marian caught the full implication and for a moment studied her nails. "Think I'll wash my hair," she said casually. "I never seem to have time for things like that, we're on the run so much." She stood,

yawning and stretching, an unfortunate posture because it caused the uptilting cones of her breasts to
extend invitingly beneath the sweater. "More coffee,
you guys?"

Silence.

"Well, take care. I'll be in the bathroom, soaping
the locks." She chuckled, the sound dying quickly
as she turned to leave.

Lubeck caught her from behind before she had
taken three steps. His arms closed around her, hands
clutching her breasts. "Jesus God!" he said. "What
a prize! Tony must be off his nut."

"Yeah, well there's plenty for both of us," said
Rosen, approaching and resting a heavy, stroking
hand on her buttocks. "Don't hog it all, Lubeck."

"Listen you fellows," Marian whined, "Tony will
kill you. When I tell him, he'll tear you apart. Don't
you understand? He was just kidding! Honest, you
don't know him like I do. That was just his crude
way of making a little joke. Sure, he's mad at me,"
she hurried on, selling them desperately, "but he'll
realize when he gets two blocks away that none of
this is my fault. Then he'll come roaring back, ready
to apologize. You better not let him find you mauling me like this. Please!"

"On the way home tonight," said Rosen, still stroking her body, "did you see what I saw in the mirror,
Earl?"

"You kidding? You damn near broke a rib when
you nudged me. I saw it all right. This one is hot.
I mean she's an all-roads, no-brakes, got-to-have-it,
crazy-for-it chick. Man, I thought if she didn't stop
with Tony, I was gonna scream. I mean, the pain
was delicious, but unbearable, you know?"

"I know, I know, I know," chanted Roesn. "I only
met one like her. A little redhead in Brooklyn, years

ago. She got a bang outta the whole gang. You dig?"

"I dig." Lubeck hoisted the sweater. "Like this one, she had to have men. Men, men, men!"

"And that lets you bastards out!" Marian snarled. "Now let me go!" She wiggled frantically.

"Did you ever notice," said Rosen, "how a dame will take pleasure in throwing it at you when she knows you can't get to 'er?"

"Yeah, yeah," agreed Lubeck. "All this time she's been snaking around the house, tempting us. She serves it up on the table, then she grabs it away and puts it back in the Deep-freeze with big Tony to guard it. Well, Tony's gone, baby. And he left the lock off the goody box. So you got no choice. Either you play it cool and you don't get hurt, or we do it this way!"

Twisting her arm behind her until her face became contorted and ugly, he gave her bra a mighty downward wrench. It came apart and fell to the floor.

Uncaged, like great white doves taking flight, her breasts soared free. Tautly pink-nippled, impudently demanding, they rose and fell, beckoning in the quick current of her breathing.

"Holy God, what a woman!" said Rosen in a voice hoarse with awe and excitement.

"They can't be real," said Lubeck, reaching to convince himself.

"My arm," groaned Marian. "Earl, you're hurting me! Please let go and I'll—I'll—"

"You will?"

She nodded vigorously. "Yes. Yes, anything you say. If you guys promise not to hurt me."

Lubeck released her. "Baby, you got a promise." He thrust an arm around her and began walking her toward the bedroom, whispering in her ear. Rosen trailed close behind.

92

At the door she turned. She had not bothered to pull down the sweater and her breasts poked out enticingly.

"Harry," she said, her features flaccid with resignation, "be a good boy and go make yourself a little drink."

Nodding in approval, Lubeck grinned outrageously. "Yeah, make yourself a good stiff drink, Harry boy." He winked. "You might need it."

"Oh, no! No you don't," Rosen protested. "Either I'm in the first act or the show don't go on."

Marian turned to Lubeck for aid, but he seemed only amused. After a moment of injured silence, she sighed and made room for Rosen to pass. He and Lubeck both entered the room.

Slowly, abjectly, Marian closed the door. But in that moment when her face was hidden, a small, twisted smile reshaped her abundant lips, a perverse gleam brightened her eyes.

Then she locked the door and bravely faced her attackers.

Lubeck grabbed the bottom of her sweater with both hands and whipped it over her head savagely. With a yank he freed her arms and now she stood half-naked before them, waiting with limp indecision, her eyes darting fearfully from one to the other.

"Remember, you promised not to hurt me," she pleaded.

"You want her?" said Lubeck to Rosen, who was sprawled on the bed, devouring Marian with obscenely bright and hungry eyes.

"You kidding?" he answered. "Send 'er over!"

Lubeck gave her a massive shove and she fell atop Rosen with a little cry of shock. Holding her in the squeezing vise of his arms, Rosen kissed her fiercely, wetly, until she moaned for air. Then he flipped her

93

over on her back and began clawing at her breasts, bending to bite at them with all the tenderness of a rabid dog.

Meanwhile, Lubeck was wrestling with the zipper of her skirt, finally wrenching it down to the limit of its track. His face a drooling portrait of lust, he hauled the skirt from her body and tossed it to the floor. He was beyond caring, was too demented for patience with her panties. He simply caught them in his paw and ripped them away.

For a moment he stood staring at the wonder of her total nakedness, at the writhing spread-eagled thighs, the beckoning arch of loins starkly revealed in the glare of light from an overhead fixture.

Staring up from the brutal embrace of Rosen to that depraved, twisted face with its relentless mouth and degenerate eyes, Marian was suddenly in a panic of fear. It was, after all, not going to be a kind of playful orgy, but a rape of bestial cruelty by two merciless animals.

With the last of her strength she pushed Rosen off and hurled herself from the bed. But Lubeck caught her easily, his laughter mocking her as she fumbled madly with the door.

"Now," he said, as he unbuckled his belt, "it's time to stop fooling around and get down to business! Eh, Rosen?"

# – TWELVE –

TONY VIANI TURNED OFF BISCAYNE and wheeled the
blue Cadillac swiftly over the long, dark finger of
the MacArthur Causeway toward Miami Beach.

He enjoyed the power and luxury of that seventy-
five hundred dollar complex of steel. It spoke of his
superior rank in the world. It was at least a pretention
to that social status for which he secretly yearned.

Tony lighted a cigarette, collapsed his cheeks and
pulled deeply. Exhaling little jets of smoke, he
squinted in thoughtful concentration. Really, he
didn't care what use Lubeck and Rosen made of the
liberty he had given them. Unless he could recover,
Marian had caused him to crap out—a total loss. Fur-
ther, he was tired of her, up to here with her. Too
much fawning, too much begging at the barren table
of his heart, gave Tony the same uncomfortable
feeling which followed when he gorged himself with
an overabundance of food. His surfeit of Marian
bordered on loathing. Tony's interests were fickle
anyway, and there had always been great wads of
money with which to purchase variety.

But in his limited circle there were so many crusty,
unpolished dames that at first Marian had seemed a
windfall. She was an attainment, her shallow refine-
ment adding to his prestige. It had never occurred to
him that in her own way she would find him just as
fascinating. More, that she would behold him as the
object of a long search for some everlastingly un-
obtainable god and, in the end, destroy the image
she had created of herself by kneeling at his feet in
whimpering admiration. For like most rock-bound

95

egocentrics, Tony demanded obedience but yawned in the face of servility.

No matter how inventively acrobatic in bed, women were much the same to Tony once all their little tricks had been displayed. There were just so many variations and Tony knew them all. Only those females he could not buy, beat or con into submission excited him, for they were mysteries still unexplored.

Anita was one of these and now there was an excuse to catch her alone and offguard, dulled by the narcotic of sleep. Maybe with a little help, Marian might disappear. Then Anita could take her place.

In truth, Tony had been finished with Marian when he left for Los Angeles. But once back in Miami, The Plan had developed in his clever mind. Anita, so well placed at Food Thrift, had unknowingly set off his chain of thought. But when she told him that Marian was secretary to the president of Proctor Drug it struck him that Marian was ready-made to furnish information, to spy in the enemy camp. Proctor would be first on the list, replacing Food Thrift, since Anita's boss was in Europe and until he returned she might be out of contact with executive decisions. Besides, Tony would have to find a way to con Wymer—unlike Marian, she wasn't going to be a willing tool.

The scheme worked beautifully. After the blasting of a Proctor drugstore, Tony had been able to anticipate every move the company employed against him. Armed with Marian's inside track, he had completely outmaneuvered Proctor and the police in the extortion of a quarter million.

Again, he might have discarded Marian. But she would be useful in the Food Thrift operation. She could pump Wymer casually, make her an unwitting spy. Furthermore, if deserted, she might talk. And finally, she offered forty-seven thousand of her husband's money as a kind of dowry. Tony was a greedy man and such a bonus delighted him.

Altogether it was a jackpot of luck to find two dames in key positions to help his plan. Spies were not necessary to carry out the scheme, but they were the best kind of insurance against failure.

Tony swerved around a lone car, relaxed against the cushioned seat and smiled. Given the signal, Lubeck and Rosen would waste little time with Marian. They would give her a romp she wouldn't forget.

Tony's sensual instincts were strange and perverse and for a minute he composed a close-up picture of Marian, nude and helpless, being ravished by his henchmen. It was a miniature reel of pornography which stirred Tony to a pitch of exquisite excitement. Perhaps later he would have his turn, too.

In any case, Marian would get the message. She was on her way out. When the Food Thrift thing was done and she had played her part, she would have to get lost in a hurry. Tony hoped his disdainful treatment of her would ease the way. If not, there were other methods. As long as he was left free to play the ever broadening field without the annoyance of her cloying possessiveness and her jealous tongue, he would be satisfied. The all-important problem was to make certain she kept her mouth shut.

Tony pulled himself out of his reverie when he reached Anita's apartment. He parked the car and strode toward the building.

She was a long time answering his summons, and even then she stood well behind the door and kept it chained.

"Who is it?" she asked sleepily.

"Who else looks like me?" Tony flashed a loose, good-natured grin and spoke thickly. He carried his coat and his tie was askew.

"Tony—my God! Listen, I'm half asleep." Her voice was pleading, though Tony knew she was secretly irritated.

"You're half asleep an' I'm half loaded. Makes us even. Been partyin' around, ya know? I'm on the way home. Left the crew at a joint couple blocks away, came over for a little chat. Got to talk to you. Important, understand?"

"Tony, have a heart." Behind the door she rubbed her eyes. "I've got to go to work in a few hours. Won't it keep?"

"Nope. Won't keep."

"I'm sorry, Tony," she said more firmly. "I can't possibly see you now. Be a good guy and call me at the office."

She began to close the door but Tony had his foot wedged.

"Anita," he said, a trace of menace altering his tone, "when Tony Viani wants conversation, he wants conversation. No little door an' no little chain is gonna stop him. C'mon now, baby. Won't take a minute."

After a nervous silence she said, "All right, Tony. I see you're determined."

Tony smiled and removed his foot. "That's a girl, that's my good little girl."

"Just gave me a few seconds to put on a robe and comb my hair."

"Well now, I could wait inside and—"

But she had quickly closed the door.

# – THIRTEEN –

FOR A MOMENT Anita leaned against the other side of the door listening, breathing rapidly. Then she raced on tiptoe into the bedroom. The hotel number Warren Emrick had given her so that she could keep him posted was on the back of an envelope by the phone. She dialed swiftly, asked for Mr. Bradford, the name Warren was still using as a cover. He sounded wide awake.

"Warren, it's Anita."

"Funny—I couldn't sleep and I was just thinking about you."

"Not so funny. Tony's here!"

"There?"

"Outside the door. I'm stalling him but I've got to let him in because he won't go away. Listen, I'm scared silly of that man. He pretends it's just a friendly little call, but I know him, there's something terrible on his mind. He can't keep it out of his eyes, for all his sick smiles. I think he's been home and found that money missing and he suspects I know something. Lord, what shall I do? Even if there was a reason, I couldn't call the police because of my brother. He may be involved with Tony."

"No, don't call the police. Just go on stalling him. I'll be right over!"

"Don't be insane, Warren. He'd kill you!"

"Do what I say! Stall! Now hang up so I can get started."

"It's impossible to stall him much longer, he'd break the door down. I'll have to let him in. So if you must come over, just stay near but keep out of sight. I'll leave the door unlocked and if I need you, I've got good lungs. Otherwise—please, please don't get mixed up in this! Promise?"

"Okay, okay. Don't excite him, pretend to play ball. I'm on the way!"

She heard the receiver fall heavily.

Quickly Anita crossed to the closet and removed her blue negligée. She draped it tightly around her and hurried to the bathroom. She had made three passes with the comb when she heard Tony pounding on the door. She paused, chewed her lip, and continued combing. When Tony's fist threatened to splinter the wood, she dropped the comb and went to let him in.

"Thought you fell asleep," he said, grinning savagely. He stepped into the living room and tossed his coat over a chair.

While his back was turned, Anita released the lock and closed the door. "You know women, Tony. Even at four in the morning they have to preen for a man. It's a matter of pride."

"I like a woman with pride," Tony agreed, though everything he said had an undertone of malice. "One thing I can't take is a dame who slobbers all over a man. No pride, no guts." He sat down heavily on the sofa.

Anita prepared to take a seat opposite him but he motioned her imperiously to sit beside him on the sofa. She hesitated, then obeyed, keeping a space between them.

Tony swung to face her, the pretense of semi-drunkenness gone from his manner.

"How was the party?" he inquired, slit-eyed behind the swirl of smoke from the cigarette he was lighting.

"A bore. Terrible bore. Wish I'd chucked it all and gone along with you."

"Yeah? We had a ball, that's for sure. You just get in?"

"Not long ago. Couple of hours, I guess. It is late, Tony. What did you want to see me about?"

"In time, in time. Been wanting to talk with you, kiddo. Never have a chance. We should get to know each other better. Might be profitable. You know—fun and profit."

"It's been profitable, Tony. You've done a lot for me."

"What about the fun?"

"We've had fun, haven't we?"

"Come off it! You're not talking to a school kid."

"Well, I'm not quite as broadminded as some people might like me to be," she said cautiously.

"I'm always *broad*-minded," Tony answered with a low, insinuating chuckle. He moved closer and dropped an arm around her shoulder. With an effort she kept her smile from fading completely.

"You know, I like you, sweetheart," he continued. "I could find a real soft spot for you—if I could trust you. No work, all play, bundles of cash to buy pretty toys with—if I could trust you. Can I trust you, Anita?"

"Certainly you can, Tony. After all, I have reason to be grateful to you."

"Yeah? How grateful?" His hand slipped down to cup her breast.

"Not that grateful!" she said, wrenching at his big paw. But his fingers were steel coils tightening, then groping inside her negligée. Suddenly his other hand reached out and pulled the gown free while the fingers lifted until one marvelously conical breast was exposed, dipping gently, then rising to a saucy tip.

Immobilized by shock and an oddly ambivalent mixture of desire and revulsion, she watched as his head bent sharply and she felt the hard, moist press of mouth and tongue encircling her nipple.

Then she struck him across the upturned side of his face with all her might.

101

For a moment he seemed unaware. Then he lifted his head and said with his savage grin, "That was a mistake, baby, a big mistake."

He caught her hair and cocked a giant fist to smash her face. For three frightful heartbeats he held the fist poised. Then he laughed harshly and released her.

"As I told you, kiddo, I like a dame with pride. We'll get along fine."

"No we won't," she snapped, covering herself. "You'd better leave. On your way, Tony. And I *mean* it!"

Tony moved apart from her slightly, his granite features closed, his remorseless eyes appraising her. "Keep cool," he said. "I didn't come for this. I got other things on my mind."

He plucked his cigarette from a tray and pushed long ribbons of smoke from his nose.

"When Emrick came around today," he said softly, "what did you tell him?"

Anita was not entirely unprepared. Still, her mind spun for an answer. Did he know? Or was he merely guessing?

"When *who* came around, Tony?"

"Warren Emrick! Don't try to snow me, I'm way ahead of you!"

"Warren Emrick? Marian's husband?"

"It's a lousy act, baby. It stinks! You tell me the truth and no harm done. Can you help it if he comes hunting for Marian? Just tell me what he wanted, that's all."

She hesitated, seconds too long. He read the lie on her face. Anyway, even if he weren't sure, he would beat it out of her and she wasn't brave enough to take his kind of brutal punishment. Better to admit just as little as she could and still sound convincing.

"You're right, Tony. Can I stop him from asking questions? I kept it from you because I didn't want to be in the middle. It's none of my business."

"Yeah, well I'm making it *my* business, lover-girl. What did he want?"

"Naturally, he wanted to know where he could find Marian."

Tony aimed his gaze at her. "And you said?"

"I said I didn't have an idea in the world, that I hadn't seen her in years, though I did get a letter from her now and then."

"How'd he track you down?"

"He called Burkholtz Title where Marian and I used to work. They gave him my name as an old friend. One of the girls over there, Alice Zimmerman, told me about it later. He phoned me at Food Thrift and I played dumb. But he didn't believe me. He flew down from New York and came right over here."

"But you kept the lid on, huh? You didn't give him a clue?"

"Of course not. Why should I give Marian away? She's a friend. We're all friends, aren't we?"

"I'll let you know later. So if you kept your mouth shut, how'd the bastard find my house?"

Anita made a show of surprise. "If he found your house it wasn't because of anything I told him."

"You're a goddamn liar!" Tony growled. Furiously he ground his cigarette in a tray. He rose, standing over here. "Tell me, Anita, how's Randy gettin' along these days?"

"Is that supposed to mean something sinister, Tony? He *was* keeping out of trouble. But I saw him leaving your place a few days ago, Tony. And believe me, I hope it wasn't business—just a friendly call, as he claims."

"You want him to stay sweet-smelling, don't ya?" Tony leaned closer.

"Yes, Tony, that's what I want. More than anything right now, I want Randy kept free of the wrong influence."

Tony shoved a finger under her nose. "Don't

103

gimme that Mother Superior crap! Didn't I practically bust him outta jail when they were ready
to throw away the key?"

"Yes, yes! And he's married to a sweet girl, making
an honest living now. He worships you, Tony. Don't
change him back to what he was."

"Okay. Then you tell me how Emrick got my
address! I checked, you're the only one could have
clued him."

She peered up at him gravely. "All right. But
Tony, how do you expect me to get anything straight
while you're towering over me, nearly scaring me
to death? Please sit down until I'm finished. Oh,
please, Tony!" She felt the tears brim her eyes.

Tony sat rigidly, like a stone god. "C'mon c'mon,
I'm in a hurry!"

"Well, when I wouldn't admit I knew anything
he, Mr. Emrick, started taking the place apart, going
through drawers. And he found my address book in
the desk over there."

"You just let him work your place over, huh?"

"Could I stop him? Should I have called the police?
You think he'd have let me take two steps toward
the phone? And he was watching me, I couldn't
escape."

"My address was in your book?"

"Yes."

Tony was silent, his face storming. "So he went
to the house and he broke in and stole the money.
Then what? What did he do with it?"

"What money, Tony?"

But Tony had really been talking to himself. Again
he stood. He began to pace the room. Pausing, he
hovered above her. "Where is this Emrick now, huh?
He's got to hole up somewhere. Did he say anything
that might give us a lead? He mention some hotel?
Think! He had no reason to be afraid of you, so
maybe he dropped a hint. What was it? Think, *think!*"

"Tony—you're reaching for something that isn't there. Why should he tell me anything about himself?"

"Because you're a sharp-lookin' babe and guys open up to dames like you."

"I'm sorry, Tony. Nothing."

"Well, goddamn it, I'll find the sonofabitch if I have to call every hotel in town! You got a phone book? Where's the goddamn phone?"

"Tony, he might be staying with friends, or at a motel—anyplace! Besides, there must be two hundred hotels. Are you going to call them all?"

She was stalling him desperately—he musn't use the phone because the envelope with Warren's number was beside it!

"Listen," said Tony, "you protectin' this guy? I'll call a thousand hotels if I have to. Damn right! Now where's the phone?" His eyes roved the room, he began to move away.

"I'll show you!" cried Anita, rising quickly, hoping to hide the envelope before he saw it. But he had not waited for directions, he had clumped down the little hall to find the phone himself.

He was gone too long. When he came back with the envelope in his hand, she felt as if all the blood were leaving her body, being sucked away in a vacuum of fear. Jumbled, fragmentary explanations hurtled unprocessed through her mind. Her brain was a crazy teletype out of control, sending a word-jam of bulletins.

"What's this!" Tony snarled, waving the envelope in her face. "Gold Coast Hotel, it says, and a number. Maybe Warren Emrick, eh? He told you to call him, didn't he? You're in with that bastard!"

Again he caught her hair. He yanked her head back and brought his eyes within inches of hers. "Anita, this is Tony Viani. Don't cross me, baby. You do and you'll have a very bad accident. You do

105

and I'll crucify your brother. I'll drop him into a sewer he'll never climb out of. I'll drown him in trouble. I got him out and I can put him back in— for keeps! So you play it smart, baby. Now what's this number you got here, Gold Coast Hotel?"

All this time she had been searching frantically, the mad scramble of her thoughts at last offering up one sane deception.

"Tony, you never gave me time to explain. That number is meaningless to you. A man came into our office to see Mr. Carling, the General Manager—he's my boss. We got to talking and this guy said he was one of the owners of the Gold Coast. He asked me if I'd like a job as a hostess there. I said I wasn't interested, but this man insisted I take his number. That's all there is to it, Tony."

*Thank God*, she thought, *I didn't put Warren's name on that envelope!*

Tony's eyes were evil microscopes, examining her, probing for the lie. But at last, he let her go. He dropped the envelope at her feet and crossed to the door.

He turned. "You think I'd take your word for it? I dialed that number right off, checked with the hotel. No Warren Emrick. But he could have been using a phony name. If you hear from Emrick, you find out where he is, con it out of him. Then you get hold of me on the double. Understand?"

"Sure, Tony. I'll call you right away."

"So long, baby. For the time being, you still got a friend."

He went out.

# – FOURTEEN –

WARREN EMRICK HAD ARRIVED just about the time Tony began to shout his threats. With an ear pressed to Anita's door it was not difficult to follow at least the implications of the conversation. In those last moments, when it was clear that Tony was leaving, Warren ducked down the hall, out of sight.

From his concealment, Warren was able to glimpse Tony's broad retreating back. He was impressed with Tony's muscular bulk. He had the massive hardness and arrogant physical grace of a fighter.

Warren was a man accustomed to sizing up an opponent at a glance. He was not dismayed. Tony had more girth and weight but they were of equal height, and big apes fell just as surely as puny weaklings. If you understood that, given a reasonable equality of stature, skill, not size, determined the outcome. Yet Tony was governed by the laws of the jungle. He would obey only one set of rules—his own.

Warren gained the street by the back stairs just in time to see Tony fold himself into the Cadillac and pull away.

Warren quickly got the rented Chevy in motion and followed at a discreet distance. Traffic was light at the hour and it was necessary to remain well behind.

Warren did not want Viani to observe his tail. Not yet, not while Tony could be certain that he had picked up his shadow at Anita Wymer's apartment house. There should not be a definite connection which would endanger Anita.

To insure against the possibility, Warren followed distantly until he was quite positive that Viani was returning home. Then he raced over another route toward the toll gates of Biscayne Key. Tony could not reach the Key without taking the toll road. And since Viani was driving at a normal pace, with any luck at all Warren should arrive first.

He was, in fact, a good three minutes ahead. When the Cadillac passed through the gate Warren was waiting a quarter mile beyond, hidden amongst the palms at the edge of the bay.

The moment the Cadillac whirled past, Warren flipped on his lights and overtook Viani rapidly. For two miles he glued himself to Viani's tail. When the Cadillac picked up speed, he closed the distance. When it slowed, he slowed. When it turned, he turned.

Viani got the drift. He gunned forward and braked suddenly. Then he adjusted the rear-view mirror for a better look. Once, he swung his big head around to glare challengingly into the hard beam of Warren's lights.

At last Viani veered from the main road and entered one of the dark, deserted parking lots behind a public beach. Grinning, Warren followed. As expected, Tony had led him to the logical, the perfect arena.

The Cadillac cut sharply left and sailed down one of the parking aisles, halting abruptly near the moon-gold rim of the beach. Its lights flared briefly, white-washing the sand, creating palm trees from shadows, giving substance to tables and benches, charcoal grills, rest rooms and food stands. Then the lights went off and there was only a black abyss.

Warren approached swiftly, before Tony could take advantage of a hiding place. The Chevy beams caught Tony alighting, moving around the Cadillac to put metal between them. But at the last second

108

Warren swerved neatly to the side of the big sedan where Tony had taken cover. Pinning him with the headlights as he braked, Warren grabbed the stubby .38 revolver which he had placed on the seat beside him and extended it out the window at Viani.

Tony was leaning against the door of his car, one hand in his pocket, a look of wary insolence carved on his face.

"Hold it right there, Viani! Bring that gun out of your pocket by the barrel—nice and slow, like a smart boy—then heave it over here."

Tony did not seem very disturbed. His hand remained in his pocket. Softly he asked, "Who are you, buddy? Cop? You got credentials, bring 'em here and I'll let you have the iron."

"You want credentials, I'll send you six of them right out of the barrel of this thirty-eight. Now cut the crap and toss that gun over here just the way I told you!"

Tony's hand fumbled inside the pocket, the barrel of a blue-steel automatic appeared slowly. Tony gave the gun a disdainful toss and it landed with a metallic thud beside the Chevy. Warren got out of the car cautiously, retrieved the gun, held it in his other hand.

"You're lucky, wise guy," said Tony. "I thought you were a cop just makin' a little pinch or I woulda plugged you before. Lights blinded me so I couldn't tell."

"What makes you think I'm not a cop, Tony-boy?"

"Where's the radio rig on that wagon? You don't smell like cop, either. You stink like a small-time punk. Now what you want—dough? I got a little roll here you can borrow 'til I catch up with you. Take it and get lost while you can still hide behind those cannons."

"Would you like to know who I am, Tony?"

109

"Suit yourself. I'll find out sooner or later. I'm gonna hunt you down and take you apart in sections, Buster."

"We're old friends, Tony-boy. I'm Warren Emrick."

Tony leaned forward, squinting against the glare. He began to chuckle, though it sounded more like growling.

"Now that takes real nerve, bastard. You steal the whole bundle, then *you* come lookin' for *me*." He took a step forward and the grin on his face could only be described as weird. "Well, you got about ten seconds to blast me before I take those toys away and ram 'em up your nose!"

Warren backed off to a grassy palm-strewn patch that bordered the beach. He beckoned, but Viani was already moving toward him slowly.

"You want these guns, Tony? It's easy. All you got to do now is come and get 'em. C'mon, Tony-boy. Show me what a big, brave, wife-stealing sonofabitch you are!"

"Jesus God," Viani sneered. "This is gonna be the most fun I ever had in my whole life!"

He came on easily with the weird grin painted across his face; long arms dangling at his sides, mocking the need of defense; a great jagged rock of a man looming up in the pale moonlight.

Warren wasn't there when that knotty club of a fist came hurtling up to cave in his face. He danced lightly to one side and explored Tony's bone-hard profile with two sharp piston jabs that rocked his head and threw him off balance. Warren followed with a body-powered right that crashed solidly against the side of Viani's jaw, gouging flesh and chipping bone, drawing the first blood.

Viani staggered, recovered without a sound of complaint. But when he swung about, there was new respect in his protective stance. Crouching, he stepped in cautiously, ducked a left and plunged a heaving right into Warren's middle. As Warren bent in pain, Tony quickly grasped him behind the head, yanked down and tried to crush Warren's face on his lifting sledge of a knee.

It was an old trick and Warren saved himself by a mighty side-thrust of his body, at the same time elbowing Tony in the mouth.

Tony snarled in anger and, when Warren came about, aimed a terrible kick to his groin. Warren bent out of range, caught the foot at chest level and twisted until Tony fell awkwardly to the ground.

He stood over Tony; the temptation to boot his head like a football was almost unbearable.

"Get up, get up, you sneaky bastard! Or I'll step on your face and squash you like a greasy bug!"

Tony crouched to rise, then dived at Warren's legs. Warren fell hard, with Tony swarming all over him. He saw Tony's fist pile-driving downward at his face. He shifted his head, but not fast enough. The blow hammered his brow thunderously, then glanced off.

For a moment the night faded into deeper darkness, then cleared again just as Tony's other fist was held aloft for that precise delivery that would end the fight and probably Warren's life.

Warren rolled desperately, swung his arm over his head and took the pounding on his shoulder. Now he rolled back again, at the same time arching his fist upward and catching Tony squarely on the Adam's apple. Viani choked, grasped his throat. Warren bounced up, blood pouring into his left eye, blinding him. Tony was barely standing when he clobbered him down again with such tremendous drive that he felt the bones of his knuckles splinter.

Viani gurgled, spitting teeth and red drool. He seemed to understand neither pain nor fear, for he

111

was up again instantly, his eyes wildly dilated with fury. Head down, he bulled forward. Warren stepped aside and chopped his ear. Tony weaved, but continued his course, gaining speed.

Too late, Warren saw that he was making for the guns which lay a few feet beyond. Tony fell upon them, got his fingers around the automatic and whirled. He took aim and fired at Warren's plunging figure. The shot barked at the night, breaking its silence into echoing fragments. Warren hardly felt the bullet sear his hip. He was already launching his foot for the kick when the second shot blasted from the muzzle, thrusting a thin finger of yellow-orange flame toward the sky two inches left of Warren's head.

Shoe leather and flesh came together with a meaty sound. Viani fell backward like a stone. For seconds, as Warren took the gun from his limp hand, he lay in a crimson wash of his own blood. Then, astonishingly, he began to hoist himself agonizingly to a sitting, then a kneeling position. Apparently unable to stand, he looked up at Warren, his battered grotesque face slashed by an obscene, blood-smeared grin.

"You—you wait," he said moistly. "You got twenty-four hours. Then I'm gonna kill ya. Last—last thing I ever do, I'm gonna hunt ya down and watch you die!"

Abruptly he stood, stumbled toward Warren, his chest heaving, sinewy biceps bulging from the fragments of his sport shirt. He lunged a big ham at Warren, the blow powerful but inept. Warren dodged it easily. Then Viani stood gasping, his eyes fogged and staring.

"Oh, you poor dumb bastard," Warren murmured. "So long, lover-boy." And with that he cocked his fist, measured the target with his good eye, and buckled Tony's nose with a sickening wham that toppled him slowly backward until he fell in a thumping heap of oblivion.

For a few moments Warren leaned over Viani, staring down at the wreck of his features. Then he worked his mouth and spat carefully in Tony's face.

He scooped the weapons from the ground and walked wearily back to the Chevy. He climbed in and wound the motor to life.

For a time he sat contemplating the fallen body of Tony Viani. *Not bad for a city boy*, he thought. *Not bad at all for a desk-jockey.*

Aloud, he said, "Round two, Marian. There's a little present for you. I'll be seein' you, honey."

Then he backed and gunned away into the morning.

# – FIFTEEN –

THAT AFTERNOON, with Miami newspapers on the stands headlining the Food Thrift bomb extortion, Marian Emrick placed a casual call to Anita Wymer at her office.

"Just wanted to know how you were getting along, sweetie," said Marian. "We missed you last night—had a wing-ding 'til all hours—champagne, floor show—the works."

"Yes, I heard all about it from Tony," said Anita. "Well, maybe next time." Anita sounded pleasant though somehow remote.

"Sure," replied Marian brightly. "Just give us a few days and we'll plan something special."

"Uh-huh. Okay then . . . listen, Marian, I'm going to have to run. All hell has broken loose and I'm rather tied up at the moment."

"Oh? That's too bad, dear. Anything wrong?"

"Wrong! Didn't you read the newspapers?"

"The papers? Why, no. We got home so late, we've been sleeping all day. Now you've got me curious. Can't you tell me in one big breathless sentence?"

Anita explained briefly what Marian knew all too well.

"Dear God, what a mess!" Marian exclaimed, winking at Tony who lay supine on the couch listening, his face a patchwork of bandages. "How perfectly awful, Anita! Well, they certainly aren't going to let those—those *gangsters* get away with it, are they?"

"No, of course not," Anita answered. "Mr. Carling

114

says that Mr. Stienmetz—he's the president—is absolutely determined to catch those filthy bombers if it takes him a year and every cent he has. It's a matter of pride with him, you know. The police are on it and Mr. Stienmetz has hired private investigators, too."

"I see, I see. How very exciting to be right there on the spot, darling! No use to read the newspapers when *you* know so much more than *they* do." Again she winked broadly at Tony. "Now I won't hold you another minute but I just *have* to know. Are they actually going to be so stupid as to pay those dirty swindlers that money?"

"Marian, what else can we do?" said Anita possessively, speaking now as one flattered by this small limelight of attention. "It's a very dangerous situation," she went on, apparently having forgotten all about being in haste to get back to her work. "If we don't pay they could blow up another store—perhaps in broad daylight with customers shopping. And that would be the end, the living end, you know. We'd have no choice but to close down."

"Well, I just *hate* to see them get away with it!" said Marian indignantly. "Isn't there some way those monsters can be trapped? I mean, when they try to collect the money couldn't you people nail them then?"

"Not then," said Anita. "It's very complicated and I haven't time to explain. But we'll catch the criminals because we'll have police following their contact man, and then when he tries to deliver—oh, Lord, here comes Mr. Carling!" she said in a near whisper. "Have to go now, Marian."

"Phone you tomorrow, dear."

"Bye," said Anita, and cut the connection.

"Well . . .?" Tony growled.

115

"It looks good, Tony. They're going to pay. But they're going to tail our boy and try to nab us that way."

"Huh? Fat chance! I'm way ahead of them. What else?"

"Nothing important. Stienmetz is in an uproar and he's hiring private detectives to work on us, too."

"That's funny. Any other jokes? What's with the little pigeon? She sound suspicious?"

"Oh, she swallowed the bait beautifully. She would have gushed another ten minutes but her boss came and she had to hang up."

Tony nodded sagely, dragged on his cigarette and pondered. His swollen, disordered face seemed to have been taken apart and put back together with careless attention. His eyes appeared lost in puffy enclosures of red-purple flesh.

He glanced painfully at his watch. "Okay," he said. "Another half-hour and I'l make a call. We'll set this grab in motion. We should have it wrapped up by ten tonight."

Marian crossed to hover above him anxiously. "Oh, dear," she groaned. "You do look frightfully uncomfortable. What a cruel thing! That horrible animal. I told you Warren was a brute and you shouldn't underestimate him. How did I ever *stand* him?" She reached down and stroked Tony's head. "May I get you something, darling? Coffee? A drink?"

He brushed her hand aside and gave her a backward shove. "Take off, you bitch! Go see what you can do for Lubeck or Rosen. Yeah, they might want a little service, too, and you're just the one to service 'em. Eh, baby?"

"Tony, how can you say such things? Oh, Tony, why do you do this to me? Don't you love me any more?"

But Tony wasn't listening. He smoked silently,

116

examining some invisible plan which apparently outlined itself across the face of the ceiling.

Watching him, Marian began to cry softly. Suddenly she turned and fled from the room.

Precisely at seven that same evening a taxi entered the gates of a great, white cream puff of a mansion on the ocean at Miami Beach. The taxi circled the drive and paused at the door.

The cab was empty and after a few moments, during which the cabby gazed with curiosity at the magnificence around him, he alighted and jabbed a finger at the bell button. He did not notice the man who peered from the shrub-thick darkness beside the dwelling and who signaled to someone unseen behind him.

The door was opened immediately by a slight, gray-haired little man who wore out-sized, horn-rimmed glasses which seemed to intimidate his small features. His was the mild, studiously abstract face of the stereotype bookkeeper, hunched from a lifetime of self-effacing devotion to his musty ledgers.

"Uh, I'm supposed to ask for a Mr. Stienmetz," said the cabby.

"You're talking to him!" snapped the man with a brisk authority.

"Mr. David Stienmetz?" asked the cabby, who had been certain that he was being screened by a factotum of some sort.

"Well, what is it you want?" Stienmetz asked.

The driver screwed up his face, prodding his memory for an answer. "Uh—my name is Speedy and Mr. Greengold sent me for the samples." He chuckled, shifted his weight and looked embarrassed. "That's what I'm supposed to tell ya, anyway."

"I know all that,' said Stienmetz irritably. "Now what is your real name?"

117

"Well, sir, people just call me Buck. But it's Buckmaster, Henry Buckmaster."

"And how long have you been driving a cab for your present employers, Mr. Buckmaster?"

"Ahhh, lemme see . . ." Buckmaster consulted the stars for an answer. " 'Bout twelve years now. Yeah, it's twelve because I remember when—"

"I have no time for nostalgic reflections," said Stienmetz. "Who sent you on this errand?"

"This Mr. Greengold, like I tole ya. Ain't he a friend of yours?"

"You met the man?"

"No, sir. The call came over the radio. Dispatcher says, come out here, give you the message and pick up a brief case."

"Then what?"

"I'm supposed to hold on to it until this Greengold calls in and tells me where to bring it. I thought it was a joke, but this man is supposed to gimme fifty bucks tip when he gets the case. Now that kinda dough I take serious."

"Go back to your cab then, Buckmaster. I'll bring the brief case out to you."

"Yes, sir."

Stienmetz returned in a minute carrying a large, bulging brief case. The case was new and made of a rich tan leather. Concealed in a specially constructed pouch within the case was a tiny radio signaling device by means of which the progress of the brief case could be determined a mile away.

Stienmetz leaned in the cab window and offered up the case. "Now I want you to guard these—uh—samples carefully, Buckmaster. They have no cash value, you understand, but they can't be replaced. Don't let them out of your sight until delivery. I'm going to hold you personally responsible."

"Yes, sir. You can rest easy. They're in good hands."

Stienmetz flipped a ten dollar bill from his wallet and passed it to the cabby.

"Thank you, sir. Thanks very much! I'll take care of it, you bet!" He touched his cap and shifted into gear.

"Just a moment," said Stienmetz. He leaned inside the rear of the cab and studied the driver's framed photo. Then he peered into Buckmaster's face. "All right," he said gravely. "You can go now."

Stienmetz watched the tail lights of the taxi fade around the drive and vanish.

Instantly two men came trotting from the shadows to stand beside him.

"Got the license number, sir," said one. "It's a genuine hack all right."

"The driver is either a pawn or the world's best actor," Stienmetz observed. "Is everything set?"

"Yes, sir. The first tail will pick him up about a block away. The next in half a mile, and so on, in relays."

"Good," Stienmetz replied. "You boys have a lot going for you. I don't see how we can miss. With that radio gadget to home in on, the slimy bastards won't get far." He walked away toward the house. "Keep me informed, will you?" he called over his shoulder.

"Yes, sir. Sure will."

"I'm not going to close my eyes until they're caught, so don't hesitate to call me at any hour."

"That's a promise, Mr. Stienmetz."

"Bombs," he said. "Atom bombs and homemade bombs. A bomb for every occasion. What kind of a world is this?"

Without waiting for an answer, he turned and went into the house.

# — SIXTEEN —

ANITA WYMER CAME OUT of the kitchen with the cocktail shaker and sank down next to Warren on the sofa. She poured another round of Black Russians.

"That's four," she said. "And that's plenty. Really, I think I should fix dinner. I'm beginning to feel just a wee bit stoned."

Warren knew it was true, and he was secretly amused. He lifted his glass and drank. "I don't recommend these on an empty stomach. But they do stimulate the appetite, while promoting cordial relationships all over the place."

"I'll go whip something together," said Anita, starting to rise.

Warren withstrained her, placing a hand gently on her shoulder, allowing it to drift over her back caressingly. "Thanks," he said, "but I'm not very hungry for food. Maybe a little later."

"Warren," she said with mock severity, "when a person speaks of appetite, I usually assume they are referring to food."

Warren grinned. "Appetite is a broad word," he suggested, his arm circling her shoulders.

"I think *loose* word is a better description," Anita returned, fixing him with a scolding eye, though her lips twitched with the need to laugh. "Yes, you're becoming a loose character, Warren. The Russian influence is not good for you at all. You must confine yourself to the straight-thinking, square-shooting purity of the American martini."

"True," said Warren, "but it was your idea to go Russian. Remember?"

"I was tempted by the promise of the one we had last night."

Her expression altered, she inspected the ugly purple welt on his forehead. "Does it still hurt?" she asked.

"Not much. Not any more than that lead burn I've got on my hip. Nothing, really." He glanced at his free hand, the bandaged one. He examined it. "Now this I can feel. I think I broke a knuckle or two on that ape's skull."

"Warren, listen to me. That man is going to find you and kill you! I know him. Oh, why did you have to fight him? You should have taken the whole thing to the police."

"Money isn't a crime, even in trunk loads. I need something more. Besides, that fight was a kind of medicine. Every time this hand stabs me with a little pain, I feel better. I feel whole again. I feel almost clean. The pain reminds me that Tony Viani is nursing his wounds somewhere and he's one sorry sonofabitch who won't ever forget."

Anita gulped her drink, then put down her glass. "It's going on seven-thirty. Why do we just sit here, pretending to relax? We should be *doing* something!"

"I know," said Warren with a twisted smile. He bent and kissed her—lightly, with the intention of exploring her mood. But she responded immediately with parted lips and searching tongue. Her arm swept around him, her hand pressed the back of his neck, stroking with electric fingers.

With his good hand he slowly unfastened the buttons of her blouse, spreading it open. She helped him with the bra, her breath coming in tight little gasps. His lips followed the long rising swell of one tremulous breast, found its crest and lingered there.

He reached for her skirt and slowly hauled it back until the V formed by lush, stockinged legs and rich,

121

soft thighs was revealed to the apex, nestled in sheer, pink panties.

Abruptly she stood, buttoning her blouse, smoothing her skirt. She lighted a cigarette with a trembling hand, inhaled deeply and crossed to a window. She parted the drape and for a moment stared thoughtfully out into the night.

She turned. "Please don't misunderstand, Warren. I'm no prude. I want to make love to you. In all honesty I—I need just that kind of sensual oblivion right now. And I hardly ever meet a man I would be willing to—" She caught her breath. "But Warren, I just can't! Don't you see? I'm so tense, so frightened. This crazy thing at the office, the threat of Tony—and Randy involved in God knows what. It's simply a matter of bad timing."

"Don't apologize," said Warren. "I knew about the timing, but I got carried away."

She returned to the sofa and plucked her glass from the table. "Oh, hell—let's have another of these Russian bombs!"

"We're all but bombed out," Warren objected.

She gave him a baleful look. "Bomb is a lousy word tonight. My boss is practically sitting on one."

Warren studied her in silence, pursing his lips. He got up and paced the room. "When I read the bomb story in the papers, Anita, there was a little offbeat tune running around in my head, but I couldn't get the words. Then, when you told me that Marian called, full of curiosity, I heard it again."

"What tune? Is this a riddle?"

"Just a way of saying that I'm looking for the words to a very dirty song entitled extortion. Do you believe in coincidence?"

Anita considered. "Yes, to a degree."

"But a fantastic coincidence is so rare as to be unlikely—correct?"

122

"Correct. What're you driving at?"

"Did you know that just before Marian left Proctor Drugs her company was taken in the same kind of bomb racket?"

"No! She never said a word!"

"Well, that makes it even more suspicious. Now she's down here cozying up to you and suddenly one of your Food Thrift markets is blown to bits and the play is on again."

"Do you really think . . . ?"

"Yes, I really think. For instance, I think that you have another unlikely coincidence when you find a quarter million in Tony's suitcase, because that's exactly how much it cost Proctor to pay off the extortioners."

"My God! Why didn't you mention this before?"

"Because it was only on the edge of my mind. The pieces just now fell into place."

"What're you going to do?"

"I'm not sure," he said, rising. "But I know where I'm going to start. C'mon, let's take a little trip over to my hotel and I'll show you the most beautiful sight in the world—money!'"

# – SEVENTEEN –

HENRY BUCKMASTER CRUISED ALONG Biscayne Boulevard near 36th Street. It had begun to drizzle and that was fine with him. It should rain all the way up to his hubcaps and business would flow like water. Anyway, it was gonna be one helluva big night. Ten from Stienmetz and fifty from this Greengold joker—a sixty plus take for the tour.

He wondered about the brief case on the floor beside him. What kind of junk did it hold? Maybe he'd take a peek later. What the hell, who would know? This one was a real weirdy and he was curious, though stranger plays and players had enlivened his job.

He had read about the Food Thrift bombing with a shrug. As long as no one got hurt, what did he care if some hoods put the squeeze on a big chow-chain?

In the first sketchy account of the bombing extortion there had been no mention of David Stienmetz, and Henry Buckmaster did not have the remotest idea that he was the instrument of delivery for three hundred thousand dollars cash.

Passing 36th street, he was hailed by an elderly couple huddling under newspapers against the increasing rain. He deposited them at the Columbus Hotel and got a ten-cent tip for his trouble.

At the hotel he plucked three paunchy conventioners from beneath the doorman's umbrella and, after checking in with the dispatcher by radio-phone, hauled them to the Playboy Club near 79th. They were in a state of alcoholic good-will and let him keep the change from a fiver. Things were looking up.

Leaving the club he was flagged by two men in a

passing car, a small black sedan. He paused uncertainly as one of the men scrambled out and got into the cab. "Drop me at the Greyhound Bus Station," the man said curtly.

Buckmaster watched the black sedan swing in the other direction. Well, the guy was in a hurry or too lazy to give his friend a boost.

After a few moments of silence the man said, "Hey, Buck—you still got that brief case?"

Buckmaster glanced sharply over his shoulder. "Who're you?"

"Police," said the man, and leaned forward to exhibit his identity card.

"Yeah, I still got it," answered Buckmaster nervously. "What's up?"

"Never mind. Let's see it."

He reached for the case and handed it back. In the mirror he saw the man open it and examine the contents carefully without removing anything. He closed the case and returned it.

"We've been right behind you all the time," the man said. "And while we're tailing you, we got a little radio check on Henry Buckmaster working for us. You know what we found?"

"On me? What could you find?"

"Nothing. Not one thing. You wash clean, Buck. So keep it that way. Just do as your told, okay?"

"Sure, sure, okay. But what's it all about?"

"You'll hear in time. Now this is what we want you to do. When you get that call to make the delivery, you give three little jabs to your brake light as a signal. Got it?"

"Yeah. Three taps on the brake pedal."

"Fine. But let's say that call doesn't come, a guy just waves you down. He steps in and he says, 'I'm Greengold, gimme the samples.' In that case, you signal three long and one short. Follow me?"

"Easy. Three long and one short. It's no sweat because in this rain you go through a few puddles, you test the brakes."

"That's the idea."

"But listen, Mister. This joker is gonna gimme a fifty-clam tip. Do I get to keep it?"

In the mirror the stern face of the cop was relieved by a wry smile. "Why not? Keep the fifty. You're gonna earn it."

There was a silence. "You still wanna go to the Greyhound?"

"That's right," the cop said. "I've got a meet there."

At the depot the officer paid the fare and gave him a fifty-cent tip. "Big deal," he grinned. "It's on the expense account. Now shove off. Oh, yeah, one thing more. Don't tamper with that case. It might go off in your face."

"You mean it?"

"Well, you never can tell. Just leave it alone."

"I will. You got my word on it."

"Get moving, then. Business as usual. But remember . . ."

Buck nodded and wheeled the cab back into traffic.

The rain had diminished, then stopped altogether, though the air was sullen and laden with a fine mist. Nearly an hour had passed and Buck was wheeling his cab east on Flagler, having delivered a passenger to a suburban area west of town.

A block behind him cruised a plain gray Plymouth sedan bearing two police detectives. From time to time their radio crackled with terse commands and they responded laconically, always reporting the progress and direction of the hack containing the brief case.

"Looks like a dead end," said one of the officers, yawning. "We should have made contact by now."

"Nahh," said the driver. "Early yet. Only twenty-five after eight. Give it time, give it time. Jesus, would I ever like to be in on the finish of this one!"

"You know what the odds are, Mike?" said the other. "Six to one. Six cars to one, all playin' tag. How we gonna be in on the kill?"

"Don't sweat," cracked the driver. "We'll be there. Maybe not first, but we'll be there. There's plenty of time because the orders are to let this Greengold take us to the hideout. He might be just a flunky. Besides, who's gonna get the glory? Us?" He snorted. "The big brass will take all the bows, you'll see."

"Well, one thing for sure," said his companion, adjusting the dials of a small black box in his lap, "this baby don't lie. The dough is still in the cab. And wherever it goes, the long fat arm of the law is sure to follow." He chuckled.

"Oh, you're a goddamn poet, Larry, that's what you are. What corn!"

"Yeah," said Larry, "and my talents are wasted on you hillbillies. Didja know I went to Harvard, class of—hey! The hack is pullin' away! You're losing it. C'mon, whip this buggy along or tomorrow we'll be traffic jockeys at some grade-school crossing. *Let's go!*"

At that moment Henry Buckmaster had remembered shortly before eight he had been told by the dispatcher to pick up a fare at a Walgreen drugstore on the button of eight-thirty. The party was a Mr. Johnston and he had been most definite about the hour—exactly eight-thirty—not a minute either side.

It was nearly that time now, the drugstore was still half a mile away and Buck would have to hop to it if he didn't want a chewing-out instead of a tip.

He arrived at the drugstore less than a minute late to find his passenger waiting out front, a massive newspaper bunched under his arm. Buck blew the horn and waved. The man trotted over and Buck said, "You Mr. Johnston?"

"That's right," he answered and climbed in. He was a rather solid man of middle years, bald as an egg, except for a pepper-salt fringe of hair above the ears. He had a round face with fleshy cheeks and a bulbous nose. His eyes were vague behind glasses contained in a thick black frame. He wore a noisy, plaid sport jacket and yellow slacks.

"Take me to the Biscayne Terrace," he said, "and roll it, buddy! I pay extra for a fast trip and I'm in a hurry!"

"Do my best," said Buck, pouring it on. "I give a man what he wants if I can. That goes for a woman, too." He snickered. "A gentleman wants me on tap at a certain time, I'm there on the nose if I have to burn a bearin' doin' it."

"Yeah, yeah."

Buck cocked his head and glanced in the mirror. "You get wet in the drench awhile ago, Mr. Johnston?"

"Just a few drops on the dome," replied Mr. Johnston. "You got a head like mine, it rolls right off."

They laughed in duet. They were silent. Strangely, Mr. Johnston began to work his hands into a pair of thin white-cotton gloves.

When they were within a few blocks of the hotel, Mr. Johnston said suddenly, "You know, I think it's time we got to really know each other, Buckmaster. So let me introduce myself. My name is Greengold. That's my real name, you see?"

"Is that right?" said Buck, swallowing. "No kidding?"

"No kidding, Speedy. So now if you'll hand over the samples from Mr. Stienmetz, we'll be in business, eh?"

"Sure, sure. Okay, Mr. Greengold." But he did

nothing, except to jab his brakes lightly, repeatedly.

"C'mon, C'mon. The samples, Speedy!"

"You got somethin' for me?" said Buck slyly, watching in the mirror.

He saw Greengold fumble in his wallet and then the fifty, crisp and new, was offered to him by a gloved hand. He tucked it in his pocket, reached for the case and passed it back. Then, to make sure, he repeated the stop-light signal for the cops he knew were just behind, though he had been unable to spot them in the traffic.

Still observing in the mirror, he saw that Greengold was very busy, his head ducked over the case, now invisible on the floor. He heard the whisper of paper and wondered if the case held a pile of documents—or plans! Yeah, maybe plans for some kind of secret invention!

In any case, Greengold seemed quite satisfied. For now, as they approached the Biscayne Terrace, he had a smug little smile on his face.

The smile faded rapidly. Greengold sat on the edge of the seat, peering at the hotel intently. Then, while the cab was still rolling to the curb, he opened the door and scrambled out with the fat brief case.

"Hey!" cried Buck. "How about the fare?"

"Charge it!" Greengold snapped, moving away, his eyes searching up the boulevard. Then a real looker of a dame climbed in the cab and demanded all of Henry Buckmaster's attention.

# — EIGHTEEN —

THE BALD MAN CALLED GREENGOLD had hardly reached the walk in front of the hotel when a black Olds 88 sedan, sparkling new, came rocketing down the boulevard. It braked harshly, burning rubber, slowing as Greengold hurled the brief case through the open window onto the front seat. Then the car, driven by a man whose features were indistinguishable in the pale light, rammed ahead and was a block away in a matter of seconds.

Greengold wheeled about and ran for the lobby of the hotel as the gray Plymouth leaped after the Olds. In a moment there was the low wail, then the rising cry of a siren. But Greengold was too busy to speculate upon the outcome of the chase. For out of the corner of his eye he caught a glimpse of two men tumbling from another car, a black Ford. These men were racing at him with drawn guns and only the milling of people before the hotel entrance prevented them from shooting him down.

Greengold gained the lobby and pounded across it toward the elevator, shoving a woman aside, knocking a man to the floor. The elevator door was already closing and he shouted. But it was too late.

He changed direction without loss of stride and made for the stairway. Over his shoulder he spied the two plain-clothes policemen as they entered the lobby and took after him while, as if caught in a dream tableau of suspended animation, hotel patrons froze in a variety of startled attitudes and postures, gaping at the spectacle.

In a gasping, heaving effort to increase his lead, Greengold mounted the stairs three at a time. Just below there were shouts, the shuffle-scrape-thump of feet ascending widlly.

At the third landing he yanked the exit door and lunged into the corridor. He ploughed ahead and around a bend to room 317, the sound of pursuit now swelling behind him. Quietly he slipped inside the room and quietly closed the door, locking it with a cautious turning of the bolt to mute the action.

He listened. Hard, breathy voices argued his disappearance. One man thought he had gone to the floor above, the other decided he must have ducked into a closet or a room. They went scampering away.

Greengold gave the room light and hastened to a mirror. For a moment he stared at his reflection. Then he reached up and, grasping the edges of the flesh-colored, hair-fringed headpiece, he swiftly peeled it off. With a gloved hand he fluffed his rich crop of reddish-brown hair, then got a comb from his pocket and ordered it carefully.

Now he pulled wads of cotton from his mouth and his cheeks collapsed. He removed the glasses and the fake bulb of nose. He studied himself. Greengold had vanished and Harry Rosen grinned back at him. From a pocket he produced a small, trim mustache of a color resembling his hair. He fixed it in place with meticulous care.

He glanced at his watch, estimating that less than a minute had passed since he entered the room. Now from a closet he removed the slightly over-sized uniform of an army captain, complete with insignia and bars. He laid this on the bed and changed rapidly to the appropriate shirt and tie. The army shirt was also a bit large so that it could be worn to conceal the civilian attire beneath.

In another minute he had neatly pinned back the sport coat sleeves and trouser cuffs and had donned the uniform over his clothes. The shoes were okay; they had been picked for the job. The gimmicks of disguise were in the coat pocket of the gaudy sport jacket.

In front of the mirror he inspected himself rigidly. He pulled back his shoulders and straightened his tie. Satisfied that he was now marvelously transformed, he plucked an officer's cap from a drawer and tucked it under his arm. His eyes roved the room to make certain he had not left the smallest clue. Registering under a phony name, he had paid in advance, telling the clerk that his suitcase had been mislaid at the railroad station and he was attempting to trace it.

Rosen went to the door, stepped out and locked it behind him. He removed the gloves and folded them into his pocket. With the officer's cap still tucked under his arm, he moved briskly around the corridor toward the elevator.

He spotted the two cops immediately. They were standing to one side of the elevator bank, conferring. They looked up sharply at his approach but gave him only the barest kind of appraisal before their eyes dismissed him and they walked purposefully in the direction from which he had come.

The car arrived and he stepped aboard, turning in time to observe the cops knocking on the first of the many doors ranging the floor. Then they were shut from view and the car descended.

Activity in the lobby seemed normal enough, people going about their business without any sign of alarm. But there were too many pairs of men scattered about the room trying to appear casual. Rosen knew instinctively that they were not casual at all.

He moved easily to the exit. There, four pairs of eyes examined him from various angles. He allowed

132

himself to be taken apart thoroughly from head to toe before he placed the cap jauntily on his head and walked out into the night.

Randy Wymer, who was the driver of the black Olds madly escaping with the brief case, flew south on Biscayne Boulevard for three blocks, then careened left in a U-turn and went catapulting north.

The gray Plymouth, siren renting the night with a mournful howling, negotiated the turn and scurried after him. Another unmarked police car in full siren trailed the Plymouth. Still a third, a cruiser bearing uniformed cops, completed the chain, though other cars were converging from different directions.

Randy was enjoying himself immensely. He was a cabby before his father-in-law made him a dispatcher, and driving anything on wheels with speed and skill had been his pleasure since his first drag race at sixteen.

Now he pushed the gas pedal to the floor boards, maneuvering dangerously around those few vehicles which had not yet pulled to the curb at the sound of the onrushing sirens. Soon, as the warning established itself, the boulevard was clear for blocks ahead and it was possible for Randy to run stop lights in safety.

It had all gone smoothly enough. Before he went off duty at eight o'clock, Randy had remained at the dispatcher's microphone, setting up the delivery as per Tony's instructions. Randy had himself chosen Buckmaster because he considered Buck to be a plodding, reliable type without the imagination to figure the game or the guts to question orders departing from routine. And the fifty-buck tip would have roped in wiser men.

Randy kept Buck on an invisible chain, not letting his fares take him so far out of range that he could not be called back into the plan according to schedule. Minutes before he turned his job over to the relief man, Randy had alerted Buck for the eighty-thirty pickup of Harry Rosen as Greengold. Then Randy had walked to a spot a block away where he had parked the stolen Olds, driving it to his waiting position near the Biscayne Terrace in plenty of time.

Tony had told Randy only a part of the plan. There were many secrets withheld. But Randy's faith in Tony was unshakable. Furthermore, Tony had explained why Randy's risk was small. Even if caught he would be made to appear comparatively innocent, a mere cog ignorantly performing an assigned task. And finally, Randy was to receive five thousand for the job, more cash than he could earn in a year, after taxes. The temptation was too great.

Randy had been warned there might be a chase. He was prepared for it. But he knew it could not be a long one because every minute that passed would bring more cops to the scene, and sooner or later he would be boxed. So, as prearranged, he raced to a street not much more than a half mile from the hotel starting point. Here, with what sounded like half the police force behind him, he took a hard right and zoomed down the side street for a block and a half, then braked skiddingly to the curb.

Now he was supposed to leave the Olds and fly up an alley on foot. He had a substantial lead and it should have been no problem to escape undetected. But just as he was launching himself to the street, a nearby patrol car, which had been alerted by radio, rocked crazily around a corner and fastened him with its spotlight.

Randy paused, made the decision and pistoned frantically down the alley. Shouts followed him, then bullets started catching up with him, winging past his head, whip-snapping around him. Randy zigzagged onward, the fear of death clutching his heart, numbing his brain with shock waves of panic.

He was suddenly a terrified little boy overwhelmed by the magnitude of what was happening to him. It was not just a crazy little game of adult cops-and-robbers in which he was always smarter and faster. They were shooting at him! Those hard cruel fingers of steel were hurtling after him to poke out his life. He was a cardboard target; his frail cringing back was the bull's-eye!

"Mama, mama!" he cried without sound. "Jesus, Almighty God in Heaven, help me!" he prayed. "Just this once and I'll never—oh, I'll never—I promise, I promise, I promise!"

He ran on. A bullet stung the wall of a building, ricocheted with a frenzied whining. He ducked left, stumbled, recovered.

He heard the heavy slap of leather on pavement. But for the moment he was concealed around the corner of a white stucco house. Circling the house he crouched behind a shrub, listening. Gruff voices speculated, then hurried off on grass-muted feet, the sound diminishing.

Randy scuttled away on tiptoe, the soft sweet wind of freedom fanning his face. Gathering speed and courage, he sprinted a block between houses, veered north another block, turned east on a residential street and slowed to a brisk walk, sobbing for breath.

He came upon a pastel green apartment house of three stories and entered. He climbed to the third floor and slumped against a wall. Gasping, he removed his gloves, tucked them into a pocket and produced a key.

When he had regained his breath and ordered his clothing, he stepped across the hall to a door. For a minute he stood there, the fear-torn expression on his face undergoing a rapid change to one of casual good-cheer. Then he unlocked the door and stepped in.

135

"Hi, honey!" he called. "I'm a little late. So what's burning for dinner?"

The two uniformed cops gave up finally and returned to the black Oldsmobile. It still remained, lights burning, motor idling, door gaping. But in the interval three more police cars had arrived to illuminate the scene with an eerie red-blinking, white-fusing radiance.

"He got away!" panted one of the cops to a plainclothes detective. "What do ya make of his heap? Find anything?"

"Yeah," said the detective. "Take a look on the seat, but don't touch, there may be prints."

The uniformed cop leaned into the Olds. He spied the brief case. It lay open, yawning toward him on its side.

"What the hell," he said. "There's nothin' in it but a bunch of paper!"

"Now you're catchin' on," said the other. "The bastards stuffed it with wads of newspaper and took off with the loot. So what we got here is just a decoy. Pretty slick, huh?"

"I'll be goddamned," the patrol cop said. "They pulled a switch. But how?"

"I don't care how," replied the detective. "I wanna know who—and where. And that's what we're gonna find out, *right now*!"

The real looker of a dame who engaged Henry Buckmaster's cab at the precise moment that Harry Rosen left it was Marian Emrick.

"Loew's Theater at One Hundred-Seventieth Street," she said. "And please hurry, I don't want to miss the last show."

"Sure, sure," Buck answered. "Some night, everyone's in a hurry. But for you, lady, I'll make like a jet." His eyes flicked up to the mirror for a reaction.

But Marian's face was averted. She looked out the window and pretended not to hear. Whenever the driver made one of his bantering, familiar remarks she simulated deep preoccupation until he subsided altogether and gave his attention to the road.

Now her hand groped along the floor, found the plastic sack and moved it silently to a position near her left toe. Then she reached inside and began to unload the stacks of currency, carefully stowing them within the giant handbag which she had bought especially for this occasion. When the bag was full she hoisted her skirt and placed the remaining bills in a deep pouch which was fastened to her right inner thigh.

With a small sigh of satisfaction she leaned back and lighted a cigarette.

At the theater (chosen because it was far enough removed from the hotel to allow her plenty of time to stow the loot) she tipped Buckmaster a dollar, bought a ticket and mounted the stairs to the balcony. She sat a seat away from the only viewer in the last row—Earl Lubeck.

His trench coat was draped across the interposing seat in such a manner that she was able to fill the secret pockets of the lining in five minutes time without once taking her eyes from the screen. The rain was a bonus but anyway the nights were excessively cool that winter and a trench coat was not unreasonable.

In another minute Lubeck reached for the trench coat, folded it neatly across his arm and rose. He left the balcony and the theater without a backward glance.

As planned, Marian did nothing so suspicious as to leave the theater soon after Lubeck. She remained for the entire show, enjoying it thoroughly while munching two candy bars which she bought at intermission.

# – NINETEEN –

When Earl Lubeck entered the house on Biscayne Key, Warren and Anita Wymer observed him from the back seat of a police car. The car had been secreted in the dark driveway of a vacant cottage across the street.

"That one is Earl Lubeck," said Anita, adjusting the field glasses. "I'm positive!"

"Whoever he is," said the detective lieutenant, seated in front with his sergeant, "he's not carrying anything but a trench coat. So where's the dough? The guy in the army uniform didn't have it either."

"The one in the uniform had me fooled," said Anita. "Without these glasses I'd never have known it was Harry Rosen."

"Let's move in and take 'em," said the sergeant. "They're all there but the woman and we got a pretty good idea where she is."

"I'll bet Viani stayed home because he wasn't feeling too well," said Warren wryly. "When I spied him through the window it seemed to me he had a little head cold."

The lieutenant turned, said over his shoulder, "You sure that back door is unlocked? We can walk right in?"

"No problem," Warren answered. "They didn't have time to get that broken glass replaced, so I stuck a hand in and got the lock turned off for you. It's all set. Okay if I come along, lieutenant? I'd like to see this pinch."

"Sorry, Mr. Emrick. There might be shooting and I can't afford to have any private citizen hurt. You had your day, now you stay out of it, please."

He said to the sergeant, "All right, give the signal for the others to close in."

When the two officers sneaked inside the house by way of the unlocked Florida Room door, they found Tony Viani, Lubeck and Rosen gathered around the kitchen table, their backs turned. Rosen still wore the uniform, though he had removed the jacket, Lubeck was pulling wads of currency from some two dozen pockets in the lining of his trench coat. Viani was counting the money as fast as it was heaped before him on the table.

"Hands up and freeze where you are!" barked the lieutenant. "Police officers. Don't try anything cute, the house is surrounded!"

After a startled moment in which their backs became rigid with alarm, Rosen and Lubeck slowly began to raise their hands.

But Tony Viani whirled and fired through the pocket of his sport jacket.

The lieutenant had seen this coming and had already taken aim. Calmly he squeezed the trigger and brought Viani down with a single shot.

As other police filled the room, shoving Rosen and Lubeck against the wall, searching them, cuffing their hands behind them, the lieutenant bent over Viani.

"It's just a shoulder wound," he said. "Better call an ambulance, though. I want this punk in good shape when they send him up to Raiford for a nice twenty year vacation."

"Yeah," said the sergeant, "he'll need a vacation. It looks like someone worked him over with a bowling pin."

The lieutenant moved to the kitchen table and began to inspect the money, fingering it lovingly.

"Speaking of vacations," he grinned, "what time does the next plane leave for Rio?"

139

It was eleven-twenty. The last show was getting ready to fold at the Loew's Theater. Outside, the two detectives slouched on the front seat of the waiting police car. Anita and Warren sat in the back seat. The cabby, Henry Buckmaster, was with them.

"Any minute now," said the lieutenant. "I checked with the box office. Sure you'll recognize this cookie, Buckmaster? Oops, sorry, Mr. Emrick. I realize it might be your wife."

"No need to be sorry, lieutenant. You should hear some of the things I've called her! And it's got to be my—that woman! She wasn't there at the house when you nabbed the others, so who else could it be?"

"Oh, that was a sweet catch," said the sergeant. "There they were, all nice and cozy around the table counting the loot."

"Some haul!" the lieutenant said. "With the cash you turned in, Mr. Emrick, it's better than half a million."

"Don't forget my forty-seven thousand," Warren answered. "I didn't come down here just to bounce Viani around, though I admit it was marvelous fun."

The lieutenant swiveled his head. "Well, since we found most of that forty-seven grand tucked away in your wife's vanity case, it's got to be considered separate. You'll get it back, I'll see to that. Hell, you took us right to their cave and we owe you that much." He puffed his cigarette thoughtfully. "You have no idea who the fourth man could be—the one who suckered us with that decoy routine in the Olds?"

Warren had already made an educated guess. It had to be Randy Wymer. With his cab company connection he was a natural. Anita was wise also, the quick jab of her elbow told him so.

He said, "Sorry lieutenant. That one is a mystery."

"Not for long," the lieutenant growled. "We'll catch him, or the others will finger him."

"I hope so," Warren lied.

"They're beginning to come out," Buck said, leaning forward and peering at the people drifting from the lobby. "When I spot this babe I'll give you the word. I'd know 'er anywhere. Man, she's a real . . ." He trailed off and Warren had to chuckle.

"Well, at least we can be pretty sure what she did with the dough," said the sergeant. "She must have passed it to Lubeck in the theater after Rosen left it in Buck's cab. But so far none of those hoods will confess a damn thing. They got the money-making book and they never heard of Marian Emrick. Some joke!"

"I don't see 'er yet," said Buck nervously. "Listen, she might get lost in that crowd."

"Lieutenant," said Warren, "do me a favor, will you? If it's Marian, let me grab her for you."

The lieutenant grinned over his shoulder. "Think you can handle it alone?"

"Lieutenant, if I could handle her the way I'd like to, she'd look like she was in the same accident that caught up with Tony Viani."

"Oh, brother, you sure disconnected his wires! Okay, why not? Hop over there now and see if you can surprise hell out of her. We'll backstop. There are men at the fire exits—no one will get by them and she'll have to show in front. Go ahead."

# — TWENTY —

WARREN CLIMBED OUT and moved away to stand in the shadows just right of the marquee. People filed past, scattering in every direction, the crowd thinning to a dubious trickle.

Warren thought of Dillinger and the moll in red who betrayed him, grimly amused at the switch. Perversely he wondered if he should have worn a red tie.

Then he saw her.

She was one of the last to leave the theater. Boldly she lingered to study the posters boasting attractions to follow. She was wearing a familiar wool-knit suit, the turquoise outfit which he had bought her. It clung to her slender-waisted, jut-breasted figure.

Grudgingly, he had to admit that she was still a lot of woman. Yet the sight of her in the clothes his money had put on her back, the memory of her treachery, sickened him. Anger came in a flood to threaten his control.

Stealthily, he crept up behind her. Seeing the known contour of her head, the long concave taper of the back which so often had molded itself to the shape of his sleeping body, his fingers clenched into fists.

"Hello, Marian," he said softly.

She turned with a start, gaping in shock. "Warren!" She backed away, terror etched on her face.

His hand snaked out and shackled her wrist, twisting it.

"Warren, please! You're hurting me!"

"Call Tony," he sneered. "Call Tony-boy to protect you." He moved off, yanking her behind him.

"Warren," she sobbed, "it was all a mistake, a terrible mistake! Tony is a filthy beast and I hate him. He forced me to take the money. Listen, Warren, listen to me, darling! I would have come home but I was afraid of Tony. He kept me a prisoner. Darling, will you forgive me and take me back? I have the money. I have all of it—and more, too! I'll give you everything, every cent!"

He paused at the edge of the parking lot. He raised his arm and aimed a hungry fist at the fragile oval of her face.

"Don't, Warren!" she whimpered. "Oh, don't hit me, please don't—I'll do anything, anything!"

"You slut!" he snarled. "You slimy, whoring maggot. How I wish you were a man! How I wish they'd set aside the rules for just one lovely minute while I clobbered you ugly, while I gave you a new look, you sneaky bitch!"

He dropped his arm and stood trembling, spent. Suddenly the anger had drained out of him, leaving him empty, weary of the whole dreadful business. A wave of sadness overcame him.

"You're really pitiful, Marian," he sighed. "But there's nothing I can do now to save you, it's much too late."

He took her arm and walked her slowly to the police car. "These men are detectives from the Miami police department," he said. "I'm afraid you'll have to go along with them, Marian."

The back door was opened by the lieutenant and Warren saw that Anita had fled. Buckmaster remained. "That's her!" he whined. "She's the one took over after the bald geezer got out. She's the one all right. I'd know 'er anywhere!"

"Get right in, Miss," said the lieutenant. He climbed in after her and slammed the door. Marian was sobbing softly.

The lieutenant leaned out the window. "Come down in the morning, Mr. Emrick," he suggested. "Then we'll straighten everything out and make a full report."

"I'll be there," Warren replied. "And Lieutenant, go easy on her, will you?"

143

"Sure," he answered. "I'll do the best I can." Then he motioned to the sergeant and the car departed. His shoulders sagging, Warren watched it till it was out of sight. He turned to see Anita approaching.

She said, "I couldn't face her. I waited in your car."

He nodded and they began to cross the lot to the Chevy.

"What will you do now?" she asked. "I suppose you'll fly back home."

"Home? Where's home? No, I'll have a few details to clean up with the police. Then I think I'll stick around for about three months."

"Oh? Why three months?"

"It takes three months to get a divorce in this state. I imagine I'll have pretty good grounds, don't you?"

"Oh, the best, the very best."

They reached the car.

"There are two times I like to celebrate," Warren said. "When I'm sad and when I'm glad. I'm some of both tonight. So would you care to get slightly stoned with me?"

"Black Russians?"

"I'm a little tired of the Russians. I prefer the straight-thinking, square-shooting purity of the American martini."

She laughed. Then they got in the car. Warren wound the motor.

"Warren," she said, "about Randy . . . thanks."

"For nothing. He's not home free yet. If Viani or his rats don't squeal, the cops'll be hunting him."

He backed, drove to the street exit and braked for traffic.

"Warren, are you bitter? Very, very bitter?"

"Yes. I'm very goddamn bitter." He turned to look carefully into her eyes. He smiled. "But don't worry, I'll get over it."

He saw an opening and gunned into the swirl of traffic.